I0619021

SPELLS AND THE
SUSPICIOUSLY SILENT

A WILLIAMS WITCH MYSTERY
BOOK FIVE

ELOISE EVERHART

ALORIUM PUBLISHING

PB ISBN: 978-1-962759-04-5

Author: Eloise Everhart

Editors: Rashida Breen and Darlene Gardner

Cover design by GetCovers

CHAPTER 1

The street was quiet as I rushed forward to open the door to Bee's Bed and Breakfast, the key ready in my hand. It was well past two in the morning, and the streets were deserted. Behind me, Heather grunted as she wrestled with the wheelchair in the trunk of Chris's SUV. I unlocked the side door and pushed it open. My heart sank as I stared at the flight of stairs ahead. I had known we would need to get Heather's mom, Iris, up the steps, but it had been a long time since I had seen them in person. I had forgotten how narrow stairs were in 1920s construction.

I gulped and looked over my shoulder. Chris was leaning into the front passenger seat. Iris had her thin arms wrapped around his neck as he lifted her.

"Are you sure you don't want to come stay at my place?" I asked. "I have a lot fewer stairs for you to worry about."

"Don't you worry about me, Dani. I'll do just fine." Iris glared at me with the same green eyes as her daughter. She hadn't appreciated the offer at the hospital either. "I've spent too many nights in a bed that isn't mine already."

"It was two nights, Mom." Heather sighed as she finally

freed the wheelchair from the trunk. It clattered onto the sidewalk.

"Two nights too many." Iris readjusted her arms around Chris's neck. "Now, if you wouldn't mind getting me up those stairs. It's late enough already, and I would like to get some sleep tonight."

I held the door open wide as Chris strode toward me. I tried not to giggle at the sight. Iris wore a pink nightgown with a yellow duckie print. Her left leg, encased from hip to mid calf in a cast, stuck straight out in front of her. And she scowled the entire way, almost as if she were daring me to make the offer again.

Iris had fallen wrong and broken her femur. The doctors had wanted to keep her one more night, but she had outright refused. Poor Heather had a hard time saying no, and I had a hard time saying no to Heather. Carrying a grumpy woman up the stairs in the middle of the night was not on my bingo card for the day, but here we were.

Chris paused in the small entry hall long enough for me to dart around him and scamper up the two flights of stairs to open the door at the top. I unlocked it and pushed the door open and flicked on the light.

Iris had lived on the top floor of Bee's Bed and Breakfast for as long as I had known her. She had inherited the row of brownstones from her father and took great pride in them. That pride, mixed with her love of bees, showed in every inch of her home. The original hardwood floors shone in the dim light. Well-maintained antique furniture filled every corner, and the bee-themed art covered the walls. A hexagon bookshelf, reminiscent of a honeycomb, covered the far wall.

I darted into the room and held the door as wide as I could. The door stopped at a ninety-degree angle as it butted up against the yellow-velvet rolled-arm sofa. Chris readjusted on the small landing and walked into the room sideways, with Iris's pointed foot leading the way.

"You can put me down on the couch," Iris said.

"Are you sure?" Chris asked.

"You seem like a sweet kid, but the only man who was ever allowed in my bedroom was Mr. Bellerose, and he's been dead for fifteen years." Iris patted Chris on his shoulder.

I ducked my head to hide my smile. Only Iris would consider a forty-year-old deputy a sweet kid. It was probably because she had known him since he was a high school student.

Chris smiled weakly and moved around the couch to deposit her gently on its cushions. Heather came in after him, huffing and puffing as she lugged the wheelchair into the room.

"All right, Mom," Heather wiped beads of sweat off her forehead, as she pushed the chair over and positioned it next to Iris so she could get into it if she needed to. "Do you have your cell phone on you?"

Iris nodded.

I grabbed Chris's hand and stepped to the side. He squeezed my fingers and rubbed his thumb across the back of my hand. I flushed. Things had been going so well between us, but I felt a little bad roping him into this middle-of-the-night ordeal. While I had a hard time saying no to Heather, Chris had a hard time saying no to me.

"Is it charged?" Heather asked.

Iris pulled it out and showed it to her. "Almost a full battery."

"Okay. If you need anything—anything at all—you call me. I don't want you trying to get something off the top shelf and falling again."

"I fall once, and suddenly you're treating me like an invalid."

"Please, Mom." Heather pinched the bridge of her nose. "You have a broken leg. Just let me take care of you."

"Fine." Iris raised her hands. "I'll call you. Now, I've been poked and prodded enough for the day. I'd like to go to bed."

Heather darted around the apartment, making sure the walkways were clear, while Chris and I waited for her at the front door. She quickly set up the coffeemaker so Iris wouldn't have to struggle with it in the morning then gave her mom a quick hug before backing out of Iris's home. We trudged down the stairs, the exhaustion of the day finally hitting us as we filed out onto the sidewalk.

"Are you going to be okay?" I squeezed Heather's shoulder.

Heather was the youngest of the Bellerose kids. All of her much-older siblings had moved away, and over the years, it had fallen on her shoulders to take care of their mother, who refused to retire despite the fact that she was pushing eighty.

"I don't know." Heather sighed.

I pulled her into a hug. She slumped against me, her head resting on my shoulder. "If you need anything, call me. Don't try to do it all on your own, okay?"

Heather laughed and pulled away. "Don't worry. Unlike my mother, I know how to ask for help when I need it."

"And if you need someone to carry her back down the stairs, call me. If I can't do it, I'm sure I can rope Harrison into doing it," Chris said.

I blanched. Harrison was one of the tallest men I knew, but he was as skinny as a beanpole.

Chris chuckled. "He may look thin, but he's wiry. I've seen him move his sleeper sofa on his own. And it weighs a lot more than Iris does."

"Thank you, guys." Heather pulled us back into a quick hug. "Now, I'm headed to bed. I've got to be up in three hours to start baking."

"You know you don't have to bake," I said.

"Maybe you're right. People come in for the coffee more than the baked goods anyway." Heather yawned, stretched, then shuffled to the Bizzy Bean, aka Cafe Meow, which sat snuggled between the two sides of Bee's Bed and Breakfast, and disappeared inside.

Chris slipped his hand into mine, and we walked back to the SUV together.

"Thank you for doing this," I said.

"You know me." He pulled open the passenger-side door for me. "I'm happy to help."

I climbed in. Chris took the driver's seat and held my hand as we drove through downtown Point Pleasant toward my home. My mind was already focused on going to sleep. *I'll have to be quiet when I get in. Feels almost like I'm the teen, sneaking back into the house.* I smiled weakly. My daughter, Grace, had just turned off her lights to go to sleep when I left. Most nights she struggled with her recurring nightmares. I didn't want to disrupt what little rest she could get.

That late at night, downtown was desolate. There wasn't a single car on the roadway or pedestrian ambling down the boardwalk. For half a block, it was so quiet it felt as if we could have been the last humans on earth. As we passed Madison Street, the flashing lights of a patrol car parked outside of Abby's bistro shattered that illusion.

The hairs on the back of my neck stood up. My breath caught in my throat as the pressure at the back of my head exploded. I gasped, my hand clamping around Chris's. Every fiber of my being screamed at me to stop. "Pull over."

"Are you okay?" Chris asked.

I stared wide eyed at the patrol car. *Why is it here? My Sight only responds like this when someone has died.* I shook my head. Abby was a friend of mine. *Please be okay.*

We slowed and came to a stop over halfway through the intersection. Chris looked between me, the patrol car, and the sign that hung over the street advertising Abby's bistro, Eats and Treats. He put the car into reverse, backed up a few

5

feet, and turned onto Madison. He parked next to the patrol car and got out.

Broken glass littered the sidewalk. Bob Wright, the local sheriff, stood a few feet away talking to a man I vaguely recognized from around town. *John? I think he owns the Mosaic art shop next door.* I stumbled out of the car after Chris. He strode toward Bob, and I trailed after him, my eyes darting around the scene. The pressure in the back of my head was building again. Bright-yellow police caution tape hung across the wide-open doorway of the bistro. I craned my neck to see inside. Every table and chair had been knocked over. Silverware littered the floor. The glass globes that hung over the tables to illuminate the space had been smashed, and Abby's dessert conveyor belt lay twisted on its side.

Bob glowered at me before turning to Chris. "When you're done with your date, get back in uniform. We're going to need all hands on this one."

Chris didn't take the bait and simply nodded. Bob wasn't a fan of me to begin with, and his dislike had only grown the more murders I helped solve.

"We've got a body in here," Deputy Harrison shouted from inside the bistro.

Tears pricked my eyes. *Not Abby. Please, not Abby.* I clutched at Chris's arm, and he pulled me into a hug.

"I wonder if Abby knew the victim," John said. "Poor girl, she ran out of here like the devil himself was chasing her not too long ago."

I exhaled sharply as the weight lifted from my shoulders. There was a dead body, but it wasn't my friend. I turned my head to listen in.

"Can you tell me what you saw?" Bob flipped open a notepad.

John nodded. "Like I said, the commotion woke me up. By the time I got outside, it was over. I saw Abby running down the street in that direction. She had another girl with her."

Bob glanced over at me, and his eyes narrowed. He put his hand on John's elbow and led him away, farther down the block out of earshot. I gritted my teeth. His dislike of me was wearing on my nerves.

Chris stepped back. "I'm going to go check in with Harrison to see what he needs so I can make sure I come back with the right things, and then I'll take you home."

I nodded. "Thank you."

Chris ducked under the police tape and disappeared into the dark interior of the bistro. I hugged my arms to my body as the chill of the night seeped into my skin. Winter was fading into spring, but at this hour, it was hard to tell. The temperature was still barely above freezing once the wind chill was taken into account. Fortunately, it never got too cold on Whidbey Island. The proximity to the Pacific Ocean kept the Seattle region relatively warm in winter and helped make it bearable in the summer months.

I closed my eyes. *Abby ran away from the scene. Does that mean she's in danger?* I focused on the sensations in my body as I asked myself that question. It wasn't an exact science, but sometimes the Sight gave me insight into a situation. By how the hair on my arms stood up or the pressure in my head ebbed and flowed, I could get a sense of what was or was not important.

My teeth clattered as my whole body shivered. I sighed and stamped my feet against the pavement to warm them. It was too cold to tell the difference between a "that's important" shiver and an "it's frigid outside" shiver. *I could come back with an obsidian mirror, maybe? Using it to see into the past could be helpful. It would be so much easier if I could force a prophetic dream.*

My eyes flew open, and adrenaline surged through my body as the realization hit me. Every time I had had a

7

prophetic dream, an object belonging to the person in danger had been sitting on my nightstand. With Jessica, it had been the carved wooden bird, and with Natasha it had been her pen. I scanned the ground, looking for anything that might belong to Abby. Technically, everything inside the bistro was hers, but I didn't want to risk putting something unimportant like a menu on my nightstand and end up dreaming about the last customer who touched it.

The ground was littered with broken glass and shattered candle holders. I mumbled the words to the spell that would heighten my senses. Motes of white light swirled out of my mouth and settled over my skin. Every time I cast a spell in public, I was glad only witches could see the lights. Any other observer would only see me mumbling to myself. I clenched my fists as the last of the light settled into my skin as I prepared myself for the sudden onslaught of sensation.

Everything went up to eleven. I squinted against the brightness of the flashing police lights and forced the biting cold on my skin to the periphery. Down the block, John was still giving his statement to Bob. "I didn't get a good look at the other girl, but she didn't look familiar. I don't think she was local."

I pushed his words aside as well and focused solely on my vision. I scanned the ground, my eyes darting from object to object until my gaze landed on a small golden seashell. It was the size of my pinky nail and had a broken hook on one end. Abby frequently wore a charm bracelet. I couldn't be sure, but I was willing to bet that it was one of her charms.

I inched closer and knelt down next to it, my fingers messing with my laces as I pretended to tie my shoe. I glanced over at Bob. He had his back turned to me. Chris was still inside the bistro. My hand darted out and snagged the charm from the pavement. My breath caught in my throat, and I tipped forward as my knees went weak. Fear radiated off the charm. I threw my other hand out and caught myself inches before I fell face forward into the glass. Fortunately, my hand landed on the few bare inches of sidewalk.

"Are you all right?" Chris asked.

I looked up as he ducked under the caution tape. "Yeah. Just lost my balance for a second." I palmed the seashell and slipped it into my pocket. I didn't know how else to explain my strange behavior. He didn't know I was a witch, and I wasn't ready to tell him. Not yet, anyway.

Chris held out his hand. "Are you ready to head out?"

"I'm so sleepy. It's past my normal bedtime." I grasped onto his hand as he helped me to my feet. "You better get me home before I turn into a pumpkin."

"I've got to put this in Harrison's cruiser, and then we can head out." Chris held up an evidence bag with a bloody chef's knife inside.

I retreated to the SUV. I sank into the passenger seat and leaned my head against the door. Chris drove me home. I kept my eyes closed, with my hands shoved into my pockets. My fingers slid across the small seashell charm the entire way home. *Please work. Please let me dream about something helpful.*

CHAPTER 2

I rolled over and glared at my alarm clock as I turned it off. The seashell charm had been on my nightstand for two nights, and I hadn't had a single dream. Despite Eats and Treats being a well-loved local establishment, the break-in had barely made the news. The article was two paragraphs long, and ended with an unsatisfactory sentence—The owner, Abigail Sinclair, was unreachable for comment.

My cat, Charlie, followed me into the bathroom and sat outside the shower. Through our shared link, I could feel his disapproval. He didn't enjoy the sensation of me showering, and he liked to make sure I was aware of it. Finding out he was my familiar was amazing overall, but there were a few drawbacks—his dislike of showers, his propensity for long naps, which made me sleepy on and off throughout the day, and him being wired at odd times during the night because he had the zoomies. But that feeling of connectedness, and his unconditional love, made up for it. By the time I got out of the shower, the morning grumpiness had faded.

I hummed as I got ready for the day. Charlie bopped his head along, his tail slowly swishing behind him. He sauntered ahead of me as I moved through my routine. I grabbed my jacket and turned to find him waiting by the front door, his front paw resting on his harness, to tell me he was ready to get out for the day.

Traffic slowly built up the closer I got to downtown Point Pleasant. Every car in front of me slowed to a crawl as they passed the bistro. The windows had been boarded up, and the sidewalk in front of it had been closed and marked off with police caution tape. I studied the building out of the corner of my eye as I drove by. *Maybe the Retirees will have heard something by now? I could ask them. When I checked with them yesterday, they hadn't heard a peep.* I chewed on my lip as my thoughts trailed off. Bob was keeping this one close to his chest. So close that the Retirees, a font of gossip, knew nothing. I doubted that had really changed over the past twelve hours. If it had, they would have called me.

Sighing, I continued on my way. I parked outside the Slice of Life diner to grab a treat for Olivia's family and me. It was nice having a friend who worked across the hall from my claims-adjusting business. She didn't bring her son, Xander, into work often. He was going to be six months old in a little over a week. It was strange thinking about how much time had passed since I chose to settle down in town. He had been born the day I decided. My life was so different now than it had been back then. From unemployed to a new business, divorced to a new boyfriend, and alone to living with a cranky teenaged witch of a daughter. Thoughts of Abby flitted through my mind. *Why do I need to know what happened in the bistro? Am I letting my Sight rule me? It's unpredictable. It doesn't always mean anything.*

I shook my head and trudged inside, leaving Charlie behind with his portable, pet-friendly heater to keep him warm in the car. The diner was packed. Every table had been filled, some with regulars but a few with unfamiliar faces. The tourist season wasn't due to start until May. It was odd to see so many out-of-towners crowded around the tables and filling up every seat at the counter. A line wound around the tables and ended a few feet before the door.

The line inched forward as Willow rapidly took order after order. I was halfway to the hostess stand when the door behind me opened, letting in a draft from outside. A couple sitting at the bar glanced over their shoulders and stiffened. The man was mid fifties, with graying hair and a sturdy build. His flannel shirt stretched across his wide shoulders. Next to him, the woman was unassuming. Her chestnut-brown hair was piled into a messy bun, and she wore a plain gray dress with black knee-high riding boots. While the man glared openly at the door, the only sign of tension in the woman was her pinched mouth.

I glanced between the couple at the bar and the group that had entered behind me. It appeared to be a family of three. The man had long brown hair pulled back into a low ponytail and a neatly trimmed beard that extended down past his collarbone. There was an ease to his style. A white button-down shirt worn over tan pants with brown loafers. The woman by his side was a stark contrast. She had sharp features and light-brown hair slicked back into a sleek updo, which matched the professional air of her black skirt suit. The girl with them, who I assumed was their daughter, looked even more out of place. She was maybe sixteen, a couple years younger than my daughter, Grace. The sides of her head were shaved, but the top section had long, wavy hair. It flowed down her left side in soft, elegant curls, which seemed at odds with her heavy black eyeliner, combat boots, and strappy black dress.

The tension in the room climbed as the man from the bar surged to his feet. His wife reached out to grip his arm, but he shrugged her off and stormed across the diner, cutting straight in front of me as he made a beeline for the door.

"How dare you show your face!" the man from the bar

spat. He came to a stop inches from the newcomers, his body vibrating with rage.

"How could we not?" the other man responded. His voice matched his expression, soft and sympathetic. "Emma was important to us as well. She will be greatly missed."

Emma? Is that the name of the girl who died at the bistro? The line had frozen in front of me as everyone turned to watch the interaction. The entire diner was silent. There were no other voices. Even the silverware had stopped clinking. The only sound was the click of the woman's heels as she scurried from her place at the bar to stand next to her husband.

"If she was so important to you," the man from the bar growled, "then why did you kill her?"

The other man held his hands wide at his sides, palms facing outward. His piercing blue eyes misted. "I promise you, we want the same thing. Justice. We would never hurt Emma. She was like family."

The man from the bar's face reddened, and a vein in his forehead throbbed as he inched closer, looming over the shorter man. "Family? She wasn't your family." He thrust his finger into the long-haired man's chest. "She was *my* daughter."

I inhaled sharply and took a faltering step forward. It looked like any second punches were going to be thrown. And with how crowded the dinner was, it would be a disaster. A third man stepped in, beating me to the punch. He slid between the two men. "I understand where you are coming from. Believe me. But is this really the right time and place?"

The woman from the bar reached out and grabbed onto her husband's arm. "David, please. Let's just leave."

The tension broke. David sagged under his wife's fingers. He pushed past the long-haired man and stumbled out onto the street with his wife and the newcomer on his heels.

I glanced from my spot in the line to the newcomers and the group outside. I had to meet Olivia in half an hour at the

Humane Society and didn't have time to stop someplace else. The door was partially cracked, so I didn't have to leave the line to listen in. I murmured the words to the spell that would heighten my senses as I shuffled forward with the crowd. I half closed my eyes to avoid being blinded by the sudden brightness of the room.

Every time I cast the spell, it got a little less overwhelming. Unfortunately, the spell heightened everything, and I had to shut things down one by one until only the sense I wanted to heighten remained. I had gotten used to the jarring nature of having everything sharpened all at once and was getting faster at narrowing in on what I was searching for. I shut out the itchiness of my wool sweater and the glare of the fluorescent lights until all that remained was the sound of the conversation outside.

"How could you possibly know what I'm feeling?" David asked.

"My daughter ran away too," the man responded. "She got caught up with Cyrus. Just like your daughter. I know she was staying with him at his group home, but... she wasn't there this morning. I just want to find her."

"My daughter's dead—"

"David." There was a warning edge to his wife's voice. "Be nice."

"What's your daughter's name?" David asked.

"Victoria Young."

David sighed. "I think—"

"Dani?" Willow called my name. I jumped and turned toward her, dropping the spell.

Willow stood behind the counter. Her strawberry-blond hair was pulled into its usual messy bun, except it was messier than usual. Stray strands had broken loose and tumbled down to frame the sides of her face. Her large, red-rimmed glasses were slightly eschew because she had shoved

14

two pencils behind the same ear. I had never seen Willow look so frazzled.

"Could I get three slices of your pecan pie?" I forced a smile onto my face to help relieve the tension.

"Coming right up." She punched in my order, and I stepped to the side so the next person could be served.

I turned back to the door. The group on the sidewalk had wandered off while I spoke to Willow. The newcomers had disappeared as well. I sighed and pulled out my phone to wait.

CHAPTER 3

I followed my GPS to the Point Pleasant Humane Society. Charlie sat perched in the front passenger seat next to me, staring out the window. Through the familiar link, I sensed his mood shift from curious to skeptical as we pulled into the parking lot. While he had never been to a shelter himself, he instinctively knew what type of place this was. The sounds of dogs desperate for their *furever* homes drifted through the air. He turned to me in his seat and glowered, his ears pointing straight back.

"Don't give me that look. We talked about this." I reached over to scratch his head, but Charlie ducked under my hand. "I'm not taking anyone new home. We are here for Olivia. You like Olivia."

Charlie cocked his head to one side. His mood was shifting again, but he wasn't sure how he felt about all this. He did like Olivia. But he also didn't like to share.

"Remember how I rescued you?" I asked. "That's what she is going to do for a dog. And their life is going to be so much better because of it."

Charlie went back to glowering. He knew I was right and didn't like it.

I hooked him up to his harness and bright-orange collar, and we hopped out of the car together. Fortunately, he didn't mind the harness. The one time I tried to leave the house without it, a well-meaning lady had tried to snatch him up when he wandered a few feet away to sniff at shrubbery. She had been afraid he was running away from me. His sudden fear had made it difficult not to snap at her. Ever since, I hooked him up to a harness so no one else made that mistake.

Charlie trotted ahead, his tail held high. He strutted through the front doors of the shelter. Olivia was already there, waiting. She was dressed casually in high-waisted jeans, a flowy white V-neck shirt tucked into the front, and an oversized red-and-black cardigan overtop. Her black hair hung in tight spirals around her face. She had her husband, Zach, and their son, Xander, in tow. Seeing them all together, I could really see how Xander had taken after both of them. He had Zach's brown eyes and lanky build and his mother's dark hair and easy smile. He really was one of the cutest babies I had ever seen. And he was getting so big. If his dad was any indication, he would be over six feet before high school. He was already the size of a nine-month-old when he wasn't even six months.

Xander babbled at the sight of Charlie. My cat slowed and looked between me and the baby. He hadn't been around the few times Olivia brought her son into the office. I nodded and sent comforting thoughts through our connection. Charlie turned back to Xander and took a few steps toward the stroller. He stood on his back legs, placing his paws on either side of the attached food tray, and peered straight into Xander's eyes.

"Hi, Charlie." Olivia crouched next to the stroller. "This is my son, Xander."

Charlie leaned in and touched his nose to Xander's and then dropped back down to the ground. Through our connection, I felt awe. He had played with a lot of kittens since I got him six months ago but had never interacted with a human baby before. I smiled down at him. Like Xander, he was big for his size. He was the size of a fully grown cat and still growing. He obviously had something like Maine coon in him, because I could tell he was going to be a big cat once he was done.

"I can't believe how big Xander's gotten." I leaned over the stroller to get a better look. "He's going to be tall, just like his daddy."

"He's been growing like a weed." Zach laughed. "My mom used to joke that when I was a baby, I grew out of clothes in less than two weeks. I think this little guy is putting my record to the test."

"He just started crawling too," Olivia added. "We've got a race between him growing and us baby proofing things in reach around the house."

A woman entered the room, wearing a blue T-shirt with the Humane Society's logo over the chest and a cheery smile on her face. She had a name tag pinned above her left breast that said Felicia. "You must be my nine o'clock. Olivia?"

Olivia stood and held out her hand. "And company. This is my husband, my son, my friend, Dani, and our office mascot, Charlie. I thought it would be a good idea to bring them all in to make sure whichever dog we go home with will be a good fit for everyone."

"I love it when families do that," Felicia said. "You have no idea how many pets end up back here, through no fault of their own, because it ended up being a poor match. Are you planning on bringing the dog into the office often?"

"At least three days a week."

I squatted and scratched Charlie behind his ears. "And this little guy comes in with me sporadically, but I'm sure they'll see each other at least once a week if not more."

"So you're going to want a dog that loves people and gets

along with cats. May I pet him?" Felicia gestured toward Charlie.

"Of course," I said.

Felicia smiled and knelt to pet him. Her hands moved as she talked. "It might also be worth getting one that's already got a bit of training. Do you have your heart set on a puppy, or are you willing to look at a dog that's a little bit older today?"

Olivia and Zach exchanged a look. He'd had dogs his whole life while this would be a first for her.

"We just want a good fit," Zach said. "We were hoping they could grow up with Xander, but a year old or so wouldn't be out of the question."

Felicia stood and led us back to a small playroom. "I have just the dog for you, then. Charlie might get some of the other dogs a bit overexcited, so how about I bring her to you?"

I nodded and stepped into the room to wait. Olivia pushed the stroller in after me, and Zach took up the rear. There were four plastic chairs, with a few dog toys strewn across the floor. I took a seat in the far corner and pulled Charlie up onto my lap. He hadn't interacted with dogs before, either, and I wanted to make sure he felt safe. He turned and curled up onto my lap, resting his head against my arm and purring.

There was something about the fluorescent lights overhead and the slight tension in the room, from everyone's anticipation over meeting a new dog, that reminded me of the diner earlier that morning. *Did Abby know Emma? Is that why she was killed in the bistro?* I chewed on my lip. Ever since finding out I was a witch, I had encountered dead body after dead body. The way my Sight had responded to the crime scene pulled me in. But I didn't know where to start. I only had a first name. The news coverage had left it vague.

"Are you okay?" Olivia asked.

I blinked and shook my head to clear my thoughts. "Oh, you know me. Crime on the brain. It's got me worried about Abby."

Zach cocked his head and raised an eyebrow at his wife. She pursed her lips and sighed.

"Why do I get the feeling you know something?" I sat up straight in my chair.

"It's probably nothing." Olivia dropped her gaze.

"That doesn't sound like nothing." I tried to catch her eye, but she avoided looking directly at me. "Did something happen to her? Is she okay?"

"It's not that…" Olivia flapped her hands.

"It's going to come out eventually, Liv," Zach murmured as he reached out to grab her hand. He squeezed it reassuringly.

I looked back and forth between them. *What could be so bad Olivia doesn't want to say it?*

"It's probably nothing. I mean, it's standard practice, right?" Olivia's hands danced as she spoke. "But Bob came over while I was having dinner with my parents to update my dad on the situation, and he said… He said Abby is considered a person of interest."

"A person of interest?" My jaw dropped. "Like a suspect?"

Olivia winced and looked up. She peered at me through a curtain of her curls. "He said they ran the prints of the murder weapon, and the only ones on it were hers."

I slumped into my seat. *That doesn't make any sense. Abby wouldn't hurt a fly.*

The door opened, and Felicia stepped into the room with a golden-haired dog in tow. It had the long, shaggy coat of a golden retriever but the body and ears of something different. The ears were big and floppy alongside the dog's wide, smiling face. The dog looked like a mix between a golden retriever, a bully breed, and something else. She was adorable.

"This is Bailey. She is nine months old and knows a few commands already. She can sit"—Felicia motioned for Bailey to sit down in front of her—"shake, roll over, stay, and come." Felicia demonstrated each of the skills in turn. "She was born here. Her mom was a golden retriever, border collie mix, we think. Bailey was with a foster family for a while, but they had to move. So we know she gets along well with both cats and kids."

"Do you know what her dad was?" Zach knelt on the floor and reached out to let Bailey sniff his hand.

"We think he was a pittie," Felicia said. "But don't let that deter you. Pitties actually score in the top twenty-three percent of dogs for temperament. In fact, they frequently test better than the classic family dog of golden retrievers."

Zach nodded. "I had one growing up. She was the best dog."

Charlie peered around my arm at the large dog. At nine months, Bailey was almost full grown. She was easily three times the size of my cat, and Charlie was a big boy. I scratched Charlie behind the ears and then dropped my hand to encourage Bailey to come over to say hello.

Bailey trotted up. She slowed for the last foot and stood there, her tail wagging a mile a minute. She inched forward at my invitation and sniffed Charlie. I felt him stiffen in my arms. I sent him calming thoughts, and he slowly relaxed and then sniffed her nose back. His skepticism was back. He wasn't sure about the dog.

Zach grabbed a toy from the floor, Bailey turned back to him, and they played. She let out a joyous woof as she pranced around and tugged at the end of the rope. A grin broke out on my face. Charlie inched forward to watch her. Slowly, his skepticism faded, and he jumped from my lap to get a closer look. Bailey looked at him, the rope toy still in her mouth. She dropped the rope and then batted a ball at Charlie. He scampered back, his eyes wide, and then he lunged forward and batted the ball back to her. She woofed playfully, and then they batted the ball back and forth across the room to each other.

"She is, of course, fixed, and is up-to-date on all her shots." Felicia continued to sing Bailey's praises. Watching them play, I couldn't help but think she was right. Bailey was perfect for the office.

They played for a good twenty more minutes before Felicia took Bailey away to go nap in her kennel.

"So, what do you think?" Zach asked after they had gone.

"She's perfect," Olivia and I said in unison.

When Felicia came back, Olivia filled out an application to adopt Bailey, and then we went to go eat pie at the office.

After Olivia and company left to go back to work, the joy at meeting Bailey quickly faded. Running my own independent claims-adjusting business took a lot of work and attention to detail. The scene from the diner, combined with what Olivia had told me about Abby, flittered through my thoughts on repeat. I had a hard time focusing for the rest of the day. I spent over half an hour staring blankly at a half-finished estimate for a claim I was working on before I closed it down and switched to routine administrative tasks that didn't require so much brain power.

I didn't know if it was my intuition, my distrust of Bob, or my own bias since Abby was my friend, but I couldn't believe that she was involved. *Maybe the Retirees know something?* I glanced between the invoice I was putting together and the clock on my wall. I was going to see them tonight for another witches' school lesson. They had their fingers on the pulse of the town. It had been twenty-four hours since I last asked. I was certain they would have heard something by now.

CHAPTER 4

Betty's truck was waiting for me in the driveway of my house. The Retirees were sitting on my porch. They had really taken their promise to my gran to watch out for me seriously. I didn't know what I would have done without them there when my daughter's powers came in. Dealing with mine was scary enough. Watching Grace struggle with hers was terrifying. As I walked up my driveway, they passed a thermos back and forth as they chatted about the spring festival coming up. Betty's family had planted cherry trees downtown generations ago, and now that spring was coming, the cherry blossoms lured tourists across the Sound. It wasn't as grand as the Cherry Blossom Festival at the University of Washington, but it had a cuter, small-town feel that appealed to older couples.

I trudged up the front steps toward them. "Oh gosh, I hope you haven't been waiting long. I thought Grace would be home to let you in."

Betty scrambled to her feet first and then held her hand out to help Agnes and Sarah up. As usual, they all wore matching tracksuits. Today they were red with white puffy jackets overtop. "Her car wasn't here when we arrived," Betty said over her shoulder.

"I knocked anyway, of course," Agnes wiped her hands on her pants.

Sarah screwed the cap back onto the thermos and handed it to Betty then bent over to pick up a box at their feet. "No one answered, of course."

"But luckily it's warm enough out now that we didn't mind waiting," Betty finished.

I moved past them to unlock the front door. Charlie darted ahead of me into the house and flopped down on the couch, claiming his spot before anyone else could enter. I chuckled and carried my bag into the dining room.

The Retirees filed in after me and began unpacking the contents of the box onto the dining room table. I took a seat, collapsing against the back of the chair, and closed my eyes. *Did I miss something about Abby? Do the Retirees know she's a person of interest? How do I tell them that?* The whole situation didn't feel right. There was a weight in my stomach, but when I probed at the questions that had filtered through my thoughts throughout the day, every time I approached one that considered Abby as a suspect, the situation felt even more wrong. Abby was a victim. I knew it in my gut.

"Earth to Dani." Betty snapped her fingers a few inches from my face.

"Sorry." I bolted upright in my seat. "I'm a little distracted today."

The Retirees sat down as a group. Agnes reached out and squeezed my hand. "You want to talk about it?"

"I heard... I heard the sheriff is considering Abby a person of interest," I said.

Agnes blinked in surprise and sat back in her seat.

"This whole morning has been strange. I saw the victim's parents this morning at Slice of Life. It got tense when this other guy called Cyrus came in, and the dad outright accused him of murder."

"Cyrus is in town?" Sarah asked.

"You know Cyrus?" I inched forward in my chair.

Sarah shook her head. "I know of him."

"Abby didn't say much, but we could read between the lines." Betty crossed her arms. "That sicko is practically a cult leader."

My heart skipped a beat. *Abby was in a cult?*

"Cult leader might be a bit dramatic," Agnes said. "But not by much."

Sarah sat and placed her hands on the table, one on top of the other. "When Abby's parents got a divorce, her mother basically kidnapped her to live on the streets. That woman was unwell."

I didn't know what to make of all that. I sagged into my seat, my eyes wide and mouth open.

"Cyrus runs a group home for homeless girls and women. And they stay longer than they should because he's so charismatic," Betty continued.

"It wasn't a healthy situation, so Abby ran away to live with her dad. A few years later, her mom reached out, but it was to invite Abby to her wedding." Sarah looked between us, her eyes settling on me to see my reaction. "From what I understand, her mom married Cyrus, and they now run the halfway house together."

"Why did you call it a cult?" I asked.

"Abby's word. Not mine." Betty shrugged. "She said she got punished if Cyrus so much as thought Abby did something wrong. She never said what the punishments were. Abby doesn't really like talking about her past."

I tapped my fingers on the arms of my chair. They were right. Abby didn't talk about her past. All I knew was that she showed up one day during her senior year of high school, got herself a food truck right after graduation, and wormed her way into the community through food. That had been ten years ago. I was so wrapped up in my own world I hadn't bothered to ask more. Knowing Cyrus was some sort of cult leader made David's reaction to seeing him make sense. If Grace ran off and joined a cult, I would hate the cult leader too.

The Retirees let me sit and stew as they unpacked the rest of the box. The box was filled with rulers, tape, tongue depressors, pencils, cardboard, and other random odds and ends. I raised an eyebrow as the last of it came out. "What's all this stuff for?"

"We had an idea of how to investigate Meredith's house without going inside," Agnes said.

Something that had happened in Meredith Walker's house in 1946 cursed all our families. During our last foray to her house, we discovered that it had been marked as a place not to go by a group of Wardens of the West, who were like the KGB of the witching world. We needed to know what had happened in there in order to lift the curse but couldn't safely go in without getting attention we did not want.

Betty grinned. "It's kind of brilliant, if I say so myself."

"And complicated. Don't forget about complicated," Sarah added.

I grabbed my bag and pulled out a notebook. If it was complicated, I had a feeling I would need to take notes. "Okay, what's the idea?"

"In the notebooks Mel left you, has she talked about sympathetic magic yet?" Agnes asked.

I scrunched up my nose and mentally went through the various lessons I had picked up from my grandmother Melinda's journals. Ever since she passed, the journals had been arriving every few months, hand delivered by a mysterious benefactor. There were a lot of lessons in them. It was hard to keep track. There had been a passage about activating your Sight that involved objects that represented something else. *Did she call that sympathetic?* "I think so? But not in a lot of detail."

"The most famous type of sympathetic magic is voodoo dolls," Sarah explained as she fiddled with a stack of tongue depressors. "You make something that is a physical representation of something else, perform magic on that representation, and through the sympathetic connection it has to the real object, the real object is affected too."

"But"—Agnes grabbed the stack from Sarah's hands— "there is a conversion ratio. Part of the power of the effect you're trying to perform is lost in translation. For anything big, you need to cast it as a circle because a normal person would cast themselves into exhaustion before successfully impacting the target."

I jotted down everything they said. It made sense, but it would take a while to wrap my head around it all.

"Unless, of course, it's a specialty of yours," Betty added.

My head jerked up at that, a smile spreading across my face. "Is it one of your specialties?"

Agnes dropped the depressors onto the table. "No."

I slumped. Nothing could be that easy.

Sarah snagged the depressors back and continued fiddling with them. "So we need to get this absolutely right and work together."

I opened a bottle of water. "So what are we going to do? Make a Meredith doll?"

Betty shook her head. "Make a Meredith dollhouse."

"We think if we can build a replica of her home, we might be able to cast a divination spell to see into the past and figure out what happened," Agnes said. "Although we might need part of the property to make it work right."

I snorted and coughed up the water I was drinking. "We have to go back in order to not go back?"

"Well, we don't need to go inside." Sarah clamped her

27

hands tightly around the tongue depressors. "Some earth from the front yard would probably do."

"Okay." I swallowed, my mouth dry, and took another sip of water. "So what's the first step?"

"Build the house," Betty said.

"But first, we need to figure out the floor plan." Agnes pulled out her own notebook and set it open on the table. "I've been trying to remember what it was like there, but I didn't see everything."

"Wasn't it built at the end of World War II?" I asked.

Sarah nodded.

I grabbed my laptop. "That's when cookie-cutter neighborhoods started. The first big one was in New York. I think it was called Levittown. But there were a few smaller-scale projects around the same time. Usually on a street level. The homes there looked similar, so it's possible they were all made with the same floor plan."

The Retirees gathered around me as I pulled up Zillow and navigated to a neighboring property. I pulled up three homes on the same street. As I suspected, they all had roughly the same interior. I grinned as I pulled up the fourth.

The front door swung open. I glanced over to see Grace shuffling into the living room, her winter coat zipped and her collar popped up to protect her neck from the cold. Almost every inch of her was covered. She wore leggings, snow boots, and her usual gloves on her hands. It was the only way she could avoid accidentally touching something and becoming overwhelmed by the emotional resonance of the item.

Grace froze in the doorway, her eyes bouncing between our faces. "It's witches' school today?"

"Yeah." I held up my notebook. "Don't worry, I've been taking notes."

Grace shuffled toward the table. She yawned and wiped at her eyes as she took a seat next to me.

"You okay?" I asked.

She nodded and rested her head on my shoulder. "It's been warming up a bit. At least during the day. I went on a walk and discovered things calm down in here"—she tapped her temple— "when I'm not surrounded by so many people. There is something about being out in nature. When sitting at an overlook, the people who were there before are almost always calm or filled with awe. It makes the feedback loops more bearable."

"That's wonderful, sweetie." I hugged her, careful not to touch her skin.

"What are you working on?" Grace asked.

"We might have figured out a way to tackle the curse problem." I handed her my notebook. "Or at least maybe figuring out how it started. We just need to build a representation of Meredith's house."

"That's cool." Grace yawned again and dropped the notebook. "I hope it works."

"I thought you would be more excited than this," I said.

Grace stretched. "Maybe I'm just tired. Being outside really settled my head, and I think I might actually get some sleep without having a nightmare. I'm trying to stay zen, and getting excited prematurely might undo all my meditations for the day."

The Retirees sat back down and began fiddling with the supplies again. If Grace could get a full night's sleep, none of us wanted to be the one to ruin it for her. She hadn't slept well in months, and it was showing. A mental fog had settled over her the past two weeks, and she struggled to remember simple things.

"I know it's early, but I'm going to grab the opportunity to rest while I can." Grace pushed herself to her feet and shuffled toward the hall. "Goodnight, Mom. I love you."

"Love you too," I said.

Grace disappeared down the hall.

I turned back to my computer and finished pulling up the last public listing from the street. Its floor plan was different, but only slightly. I flipped between the four of them. It was hard to tell if there were two models on the street or if the fourth had been renovated. "I think I'm going to have to poke around a bit more to figure out the floor plan," I said.

"And I'm going to have to buy some more glue." Sarah held up a bottle of Elmer's. Old glue had seeped out and encrusted the top. It didn't look like it was good anymore.

I helped them pack up the box, and we made plans for our next session. Before making dinner, I wrote down the details and put a note on the fridge for Grace so she wouldn't miss the next one.

After dinner, I had settled down to read in bed. I fell asleep with the book open on my chest and Charlie curled up under my arm. A tapping sound woke me up. I moved my book to the nightstand and rolled over to cuddle Charlie when there was another tap. *What was that?* I lay there with my eyes open, my ears straining for the sound to come again.

Tap.

It was a distinct sound, of something hitting glass. I sat up in bed and listened.

Tap.

It was coming from my bedroom window. I stood and shuffled over to look outside. It was a clear night, and the moon was almost full, making it easy to see Abby standing in the middle of my yard.

I scrambled back from the window and rushed down the stairs. I grabbed my coat from the back of the dining room chair and threw it on. In a matter of seconds, my legs carried me out my front door and around the side of my house. I jumped down onto the grass and ran over to Abby.

"Abby? What are you doing out here?" I pulled her into a hug.

She wasn't wearing a coat and shivered in my arms.

"You should come inside," I said.

"No." She pulled back and glanced over her shoulder at the tree line. "I can't stay long."

I studied her face. She was bare skinned, without a touch of makeup. Her short brown hair hung limply around her ears. "Are you okay? Did someone hurt you?"

Abby shook her head and grabbed my hand. "No, nobody hurt me. But… I need your help. I didn't kill Emma. You've got to believe me."

"I do." I squeezed her hand. "It's freezing out here. Come inside, and I'll do whatever I can."

Abby glanced back at the tree line again. "I can't."

"Do you know who did it?"

"I wish I did. My sister called me in a panic. I told her to wait for me at the bistro and gave her the key code to get inside. When I got there, the place was trashed, and Emma was dead." She held my gaze as she spoke. Her eyes were red rimmed, but there was an earnestness in there. Abby was pouring as much sincerity into her words as she could. She was desperate for me to believe her. And I did.

"I didn't know you had a sister." I didn't know what else to say.

"A half sister, technically," Abby smiled weakly. "Her name is Rebecca. I haven't seen her in person since she was six, but I call her at least once a month to keep in touch. You would like her." She wiped her eyes and straightened. "And we both need your help. I know you've solved multiple murder cases so far, and I've got to be honest—I have more faith in your ability to track down Emma's killer than I do in Bob."

"He might not take cases like this seriously, but not

everyone in the sheriff's department is bad. I'm sure Chris could help."

"Ask him if you want, but I can't." Abby hugged her arms to her body. "My sister needs me right now, and I can't keep her safe if Bob holds me for a few days while he figures things out. I know he's going to be upset that I didn't stick around, but... I couldn't. And he's petty enough not to care. You know that. Better than anyone."

"I..." I trailed off. Every case I had gotten involved in, it was because I stuck my nose in where it wasn't wanted. No one had ever asked me to help before.

"Dani, please." Abby gripped my hand, her eyes searching my face.

"Okay."

Abby relaxed, the smile on her face warmer. She pulled me into a hug. "Thank you, Dani. You have no idea how much this means to me."

"I'll help, but I need to know a few things."

"I'll answer what I can." Abby stepped back. "What do you need to know?"

"What was Emma's full name?" I ticked off my questions. "Why was she here? And do you have any leads?"

"Her name was Emma Wilson. Her dad is David, her mom Sophia. I don't know why she was here. Something spooked her at the group home she was staying at. I know she was there because she ran away from home. Maybe her dad found her? And as far as suspects go, I have no idea. The man who runs the group home is named Cyrus Drake, and he's not a good guy. It's possible she was running away from him. I lived with him for a while, and he could be abusive. It wouldn't surprise me if he's gotten worse." Abby glanced at the tree line again. "I'm sorry. I've been gone too long. I made the mistake of leaving my sister before, and I won't do it again. I've got to go."

Abby darted away from me into the trees. I followed her

with my eyes as far as I could until she disappeared into the darkness. I stared after her, long after she vanished. *Maybe Chris knows something. I could probably get him to help, even without telling him about my midnight visitor.* After a minute, my teeth started clattering from the cold. I wrapped my arms around myself and trudged back inside. Abby had been terrified of something. *I have to help her. She needs me.*

CHAPTER 5

I tossed and turned the rest of the night. Five a.m. came too early. I was barely awake as I went through the motions to get ready, and by five fifteen, I was out the door to meet Chris for our Miller Farm coffee date. We had been having them almost once a week since I moved to town. At first it was because I didn't want Chris to suffer alone—the sheriff had assigned him to monitor the least-used road in the entire county at an ungodly hour as punishment for helping me—but now that we were officially dating, it was one of our traditions. Very early morning coffee at the crossroads leading up to Miller's Farm.

I parked next to Chris's cruiser and scurried between the cars. I claimed the front passenger seat and handed Chris the thermos of coffee I'd made. "Good morning." I leaned over and kissed him.

He kissed me back and then smelled the coffee, inhaling deeply. "I'm so glad you convinced Heather to give you some of her roasted beans."

"It's been my best idea yet." I squeezed his hand. "So, is it all quiet on the western front?"

"Not a car in sight."

"Darn." I snapped my fingers. "I guess the cow painters are going to remain at large." For months, someone had been sneaking onto the farm and painting one of their cows blue.

"It looks like they've moved on from the cow. Now, they're egging the house."

"I wonder what the Millers did this time to deserve that."

"Not you too." He sighed. "Megan is a nice-enough lady. She doesn't deserve all the hate she gets."

I shifted in my seat. As long as I could remember, the Millers had been treated like outsiders. They rarely came into town. I had heard rumors about what started the divide, but the details always changed depending on who was telling the story. There had to be a reason the whole town hated them, though. I cleared my throat and changed the subject. "How's the investigation going for the break-in at Abby's? You guys make any headway on who might have killed that girl?"

Chris chuckled. "I wondered how long it was going to take before you asked about that."

"You can't blame a girl for being curious." I bumped him with my shoulder. "So spill the beans. How's it going?"

"Not well."

I took the thermos from Chris and sipped the coffee as I studied him out of the corner of my eye. "I heard a rumor that Abby's considered a person of interest."

"Yeah," Chris said. "It blew my mind, but she was seen fleeing the scene, and it's her prints on the murder weapon. We just can't figure out what her motive would have been. The connection between her and the victim is tenuous at best. And it seems extreme to kill someone over vandalism, you know? But all the clues lead back to her."

"I think I saw the victim's parents. David and Sophia?" I handed him back the thermos. "They were at Slice of Life yesterday. Things got a little tense, and the dad accused a man named Cyrus Drake of killing his daughter. Do you think Cyrus may have had something to do with it?"

"Maybe. We questioned him, and he was odd. Very odd. But I don't know. When we looked into him, everything came back that he's a pillar of the community. He runs a halfway house for homeless women and at-risk youth with his wife, Susan. Who just happens to be Abby's mother. It's convoluted, and loops back to Abby again. While the social worker they usually work with was out, the other ones in the office sang his praises. I mean, I know pillars of the community can be bad guys. But it's uncommon. My money would be on her father. David's never been arrested, but there are a string of reports of cops being called out on domestic violence allegations."

"Have you taken him in for questioning?" I asked.

"Not officially." Chris sighed. "Harrison is out searching for something more concrete, but so far we haven't come across any evidence that he was in town the night Emma was killed."

I sagged into my seat. "I hope you find something, because I, for one, can't picture Abby being involved at all. It baffles me that she's even considered a person of interest."

"If she came in, it would help."

"Do you think Bob would hold her in custody if she did?"

He nodded. "Until we cleared a few things. Probably not more than a day. Maybe longer if anything comes up."

I chewed my lip. If I told him about Abby's visit, he would have to report it. And her fear of being detained would come true. I couldn't risk it. My chest tightened as I lost my appetite. It would be hard keeping this from Chris, but it was for his own good. I didn't want to make him choose between his duty as a deputy and me.

"You okay?" he asked.

I shrugged and swallowed. "I just wish there was something I could do to help."

"Me too." Chris ran his fingers through his hair. "This one has us stumped. And to be honest, sometimes you notice things we don't."

"You think you could let me look inside the bistro?"

"We have cleared it." He drummed his fingers on the steering wheel. "I could let you inside, so long as I was with you."

I perked up in my seat. "Really?"

He looked between me and the time on his dashboard. "I'm only supposed to be out here for another thirty minutes before I head back into the station house. I doubt anyone is going to drive out this way, so why not? Follow me there. I can give you twenty minutes, and then I gotta go in."

"Thank you." I leaned over and kissed him then darted out of the cruiser to my car.

I followed Chris into town, buzzing with excitement the entire way. The streets were still mostly deserted by the time we arrived outside Eats and Treats Bistro. I parked next to him, grabbed a flashlight from my inspection kit in my trunk, and ducked under the police caution tape to follow him inside the building.

It was worse, and somehow better, than I originally thought. Other than the lights and the conveyor belt, nothing else appeared to be broken. But someone had taken the time to knock over every table and chair, to rip off every cushion, and to empty every cabinet and drawer in the place. At first it gave the impression of someone looking for something, but the more I stared at it, the more it looked like someone trying to give the impression of looking for something. The objects scattered across the floor were in a pattern that didn't look natural. It was hard to explain, but the room looked staged.

I walked around the space and touched a few items on the

floor. The emotions on them were muted. It was satisfaction mixed with the boredom of going through the motions, as if the last person who touched the objects was the one who cleaned them.

I eyed the twisted conveyor belt. It looked more real to me. The only things in the bistro that were truly damaged were the lights and the belt. The lights seemed practical. It would be hard for Emma to move around without being heard with the broken glass crunching underfoot. And it seemed reasonable to assume the killer would want it to be dark in here anyway. Lights might have attracted someone from the apartments across the street. The conveyor belt, though. I couldn't figure out why someone would break it other than the desire to hurt Abby. It was her pride and joy.

I inched forward and brushed my fingers along the broken machinery. I swayed on my feet as a wave of dizziness hit me. My chest tightened, and my muscles threatened to give out. I could almost see Abby as she pushed it aside. Her shock was palpable.

Shaking out my hand, I took a step back. I only had a few more minutes, and thus far, I had found nothing. Not a single thread to pull. No clues. I walked the perimeter again and stopped by the front door. The doorframe was cracked where someone had forced their way in with a crowbar. I stepped outside and examined it from another angle.

The scrapes and broken frame were almost eye level. In the few vandalism claims I had handled that had video footage, those marks always seemed to hit about mid chest. Marks this high indicated it was a tall suspect. I closed my eyes and replayed videos I had seen of people breaking in with crowbars. They were all slightly different, but there were similarities. Almost all of the vandals checked the knob to see if it was unlocked. A bunch of people would have touched the doorknob since the break-in, so that wouldn't be useful. But a lot of vandals braced themselves by touching the door or wall.

I mentally drew a line from the cracks in the doorframe to areas I expected someone to touch to brace themselves. I ran my fingers along those areas. There was a mix of different emotions, all of them muted. And then there was nothing.

Nothing.

I gasped at the strangeness of it. It was impossible that this spot had never been touched by a person before. It was a brick wall. Even if no one else had touched it, the person who originally laid the brick in place would have. Emotions lingered forever, even the unexciting ones. I had never touched an object that read as nothing before. The complete lack of emotion was strange.

Chris stepped out onto the street next to me. "Is everything all right?"

I blinked and shook out my hand. I didn't know how to explain what I had felt, so I grasped on to what I could. "It looks like whoever broke in here was tall." I pointed out the frame damage and compared it to both of our heights. "How tall was Emma?"

"Shorter than you," he said.

"Abby would have no reason to break in, and she's about my height anyway," I mused. "Which means there was at least one other person here. Someone tall, like you. Because if I was breaking into a place with a crowbar, I would put it here"—I touched the wall—"for leverage. Higher up, I would lose too much strength."

"Good catch." Chris pulled out his notepad and jotted down my impressions.

"David Wilson was tall, but Cyrus wasn't exactly short either. This could line up with either of them, to be honest."

He nodded and shoved his notepad back into this pocket.

"I've got to head into the station. Are we still on for our date later this week?"

"I wouldn't miss it." I rose up on my tippy-toes to kiss him.

Chris locked up the bistro and got into his car. I waved as he drove away and then turned on my heel to walk to the Bizzy Bean. I needed to talk to someone about the weirdness I had felt on the door, and Heather was always a good listener.

CHAPTER 6

The Bizzy Bean had only been open for twenty minutes, but there was already a line of customers out the door. Heather had the best coffee in town, so most of her regulars made sure they got in on their way to work. I caught Heather's eye, waved, and then took a seat at our usual spot at the booth in the back. The instant I sat down, Star found me. Star was Charlie's mom, and she acted as a foster mom to all the kittens that came through Heather's cat cafe. Star had a kitten dangling from her mouth, which she deposited in my lap before scampering off to corral the others. She was an excellent mom, and she trusted me to watch the more rambunctious kittens.

Muffin, the cat in my lap, had come to Heather in rough shape. When she was a newborn colony cat, something had found and attacked her. The rescue organization that had taken her in gave her enough TLC, so she was mostly healthy when she was transferred to Heather for foster care. For the first week, there were medications she had to take, and she objected strongly. Heather had the patience of a saint and made sure that the wee one still took her meds every twelve hours, like clockwork. Now that she was off the meds and could join the other kittens in the cat cafe, she was bound and determined to make up for her rough start at life by being a little hellion. The tiny kitten attacked the sleeve of my coat as I played with her. She was adorable, and someone was going to fall in love with her.

Heather collapsed into the booth across from me and slid a cup of coffee my way. She had a large cup in front of herself, which she gulped down. She yawned and rubbed at the bags under her eyes.

"Rough morning?" I put Muffin down, and she scampered off to play.

"I've been up since three a.m." Heather stared forlornly into the bottom of her cup. "I had to get up early to deal with the B and B and still have time to bake."

I raised an eyebrow at her. "I thought you weren't going to bake."

"I wasn't." She sighed. "But then I pictured how disappointed Mrs. Smith would be if she didn't get her morning scone, and I crumbled."

I laughed. "I think Mrs. Smith would understand, at least for a few days. Have you found any other help?"

"I called Linda, the intern who helped over winter break, and she's agreed to come work at the cafe on the weekends."

"That's nice of her," I said.

Heather shrugged. "I had to throw in covering the cost of the ferry. But I know she does good work, so it'll be worth it."

"How about Ash or Violet? Have your brother and sister offered to help at all?"

"Violet is out on the East Coast now and can't get the time off work. Ash has agreed to take Mom in, though. He just needs to convert his basement into a mother-in-law suite. Mom is... protesting, but he's moving forward with the renovations anyway, just in case."

"I remember after my grandfather had his stroke, Gran was at her wits' ends trying to get him to go to the right appointments instead of carrying on like nothing had happened." I took another sip of my coffee. "If I ever get that stubborn, I give you permission to slap me upside the head."

Heather grinned. "Are you sure you want to give me permission to do that? I might have to regularly."

I grinned back at her as I put my hand over my heart. "Me? Stubborn? What on earth could you be referring to?"

"You're like a bloodhound. Whenever you're on the trail of something, you don't give up until you've found it." Heather squeezed my hand. "Now, given recent events, I am almost certain you are on the trail of something. And I could really use a distraction. How's the murder investigation going?"

"Not well." I glanced around to make sure there weren't any other customers nearby. The opening rush had died down, and most of them had left already, coffee cups in hand. We had a few more minutes before the next wave hit. I leaned across the table and filled her in. I told her about what I had witnessed at the diner and Abby's late-night visit as well as the strange sensation I had encountered at the bistro.

"All right, wow." Heather leaned back into her seat and stared at me wide-eyed. "You have been up to a lot. It sounds like right now you have two lead suspects, right? Have you checked their social media?"

We made a list of suspects and potential witnesses, then pulled out our phones and began poking around online. I started with Emma's parents while Heather tackled the victim and Cyrus. David was either dull or skilled at keeping half his content behind a privacy wall. Most of his posts shared community events or baseball scores. There was nothing personal about his page. Sophia's was different. She shared cute morning videos of herself greeting the day over a cup of coffee, which showed off a sweet personality. The rest of her posts shared the same community events as her husband, with a few cute cat videos thrown into the mix. The only thing of note was she had not posted a single morning greeting since the death of her daughter, which was consistent with someone grieving. Since Emma was murdered, Sophia's only post was a check-in at a local motel, captioned with *God, give me strength.*

Heather wrinkled her nose as she scrolled, with a single eyebrow raised. She fiddled with the tip of her braid and scoffed.

"Find something interesting?" I asked.

"Have you ever encountered someone too wholesome?" Heather flipped her phone toward me. "Every single post is about him giving back to the community and loving thy neighbor. He even publicly forgave someone who carjacked him."

I flipped through the various posts and comments on his wall. Heather was right. There was nice, and then there was too nice. Cyrus was so pleasant that it was almost eerie. In every photo, he had an almost identical warm smile that never truly reached his eyes. It was unnerving. I paused over a post he had shared about his halfway home. The caption mentioned a social worker. I opened the article. It was a puff piece, praising Cyrus for his work keeping at-risk youth off the street. The article only briefly mentioned the social worker, but it noted that she had worked with Cyrus for years.

I jotted down the social worker's name as a potential character witness and handed Heather back her phone. "I'm going to find information on this social worker. Mind tackling the next person on the list?"

"Who's up next?" Heather asked.

I glanced at the notepad where we had gathered all the names. "The victim, Emma Wilson. Then Abby's mom, Susan Robertson."

Heather nodded as I dove into tracking down the social worker. I located the article again and from there followed links until I found the social worker on a professional networking site. I called her and left a voicemail asking for a meeting.

"Emma seems like she was a sweet kid." Heather glanced up from her phone as I hung up. "A sweet, somewhat-troubled kid. She didn't seem to like her dad much."

"Anything on Susan?"

"I couldn't find a profile for her, so I'm moving on to Victoria Young. That's the daughter of the guy who stopped things escalating into a fight at the cafe, isn't it?"

I nodded.

"Did you catch his name?"

"No luck," I said. "I'm hoping he's listed somewhere on Victoria's page. Most people like to list out their family members."

"She does." Heather grabbed my notebook and added Robert Young to the list. "She's older than I thought she would be. Looks like Victoria was in college."

Heather continued scrolling through the page as I pulled up Robert Young's profile. His last public post was seven years ago. Everything else was completely private. The only public-facing information was his profile picture, which was a silhouette of a man standing in front of a large aquarium tank, and the banner image, which was of a fifty-four-inch salmon. I poked around to see if I could find him on any other sites, but nothing useful came up. There were multiple dead ends, from long-abandoned social media profiles to a news story about a Robert Young perishing in a boating accident to multiple hits for either kids or elderly men with the same name. While I hadn't gotten a good look at the man I saw yesterday, I could tell the photos didn't match.

I dropped my phone onto the table and slumped in my seat, my head rolling back. "I don't think we found a single useful thing."

"So what now?"

"Talk to someone in person?" I bolted upright and grabbed my phone. "Hang on."

I pulled up Sophia's profile and located the post she'd made about the check-in. She and her husband were staying at a chain motel at the edge of town. I grabbed my purse and scooted to the edge of the booth. "They're staying in town."

"Good luck." Heather grabbed my hand and squeezed. "And stay safe. Keep me updated every step of the way."

"I promise." I crossed my heart then surged to my feet and power walked through the cafe. In two hours, I had to leave for my first home inspection. If I hurried and was very lucky, I might bump into David and Sophia Wilson at breakfast.

I pulled up to the motel and drove slowly through the parking lot. It was a three-story walk-up. I quickly looked up the motel online. It did not advertise breakfast. If the Wilsons wanted to eat, they would have to go out. I found a parking spot with a clear view of all the doors and pulled in, facing away from the building. I studied walkways through my windows and waited. Half an hour later, David walked alone out of a room on the first floor and cut across the parking lot on foot.

I scrambled out of my car and darted after him. I caught up enough to keep him in sight. He stopped at a crosswalk and waited for the light to change. I slowed my pace and timed it so I would hit the crosswalk as he was already halfway across. Keeping my pace with him, I trailed behind by about fifty paces until he entered a bar and grill. I had never been inside, but I recognized it as a local dive bar. Layers of flyers covered the windowless building. Squaring my shoulders, I followed him inside.

David had already taken a seat at the bar and had a tall glass of amber liquid in front of him. I loitered near the door, waiting for my eyes to adjust to the dim light. There was an old man at a table in the back, with an English-style breakfast half-eaten in front of him. Behind the bar was a tired-looking woman wearing an apron over a black tank top, her hair tied back in a tight ponytail.

I turned my focus back to David. His shoulders slumped, and he studied his beer more than he drank it. He tensed whenever the bartender moved in his direction. He was so jumpy. Getting him to talk was going to be a challenge. My eyes flicked between David and the bartender as I murmured the words to the relaxation potion spell. Motes of light floated out of my mouth, and I willed them toward David's drink. *Relax, so we can talk.* I finished the spell, and his drink took on a gentle glow only other witches could see.

David took another sip of his drink. The gentle glow flowed from his glass into him, settling over his skin. Once the spell took hold, I forced myself to stroll across the room and took a seat two chairs down from him. The bartender came over, and I put in an order for a Cherry Coke.

"I don't think I've seen you in here before," I said after the bartender had wandered off down the bar.

David turned his head toward me and met my gaze. "I'm only in town for a few days."

I forced a smile onto my face. "What are you in town for?"

He slumped and stared down at his beer. He picked it up and took a long swallow. "To collect my daughter's body."

"Oh my gosh." I covered my mouth with my hand to feign shock. "Are you okay? My condolences for your loss."

The bar door opened behind us, and a group of men with reflective vests tumbled into the room. The space became loud, filled with their excited voices. As a group, they converged on the bar and began animatedly giving their orders to the bartender in rapid succession. I hopped off my stool and slipped onto the one next to David.

"It feels surreal, to be honest." He swirled the contents of his glass before taking another sip. "She ran away two years ago, so in a way, she was dead to me already."

I dropped my voice and leaned in closer. "What happened?"

"She was a willful child. Always doing whatever she wanted, no matter the consequences. I lost count of the number of times I had to put my foot down and force her to focus on what was important. But she was so stubborn. Instead of going to the private school we had selected, she took off in the middle of the night."

While he talked, I rested my hand on the bar to pick up his emotional state through the wood. I could pick up the emotional resonance of whoever had touched an item last. The bar was an item, and David was currently touching the bar, so that counted as last. It wasn't perfect, but I had managed to use it to read people's emotions in real time a few times before. Unfortunately, half the group of men down the bar were also touching the bar. Excitement flowed through me in waves. I tried to hide my disappointment as I picked up my hand from the bar. With so many people touching the bar, that trick was useless. All I had to go on were David's words, and reading between the lines, he sounded controlling and like he had anger issues.

"My daughter's stubborn too," I said. "Whenever we have a fight, I try to remind myself that she loves me. I can't imagine what you are going through, though. Not being able to reconcile must be hard."

"Reconciliation takes two," he said, his voice devoid of emotion. It was almost like he was reciting an old lesson. "And has to be earned."

He downed the last of his beer, the glow of the potion fading from his skin. I gritted my teeth. It was frustrating how inconsistent that spell was. Sometimes it lasted the entire conversation, and sometimes it passed too quickly to be useful. *Does metabolism affect the duration? I wonder if there's a way to strengthen it.*

I blinked and refocused on David.

"It's felt like a dream ever since we got the call," he said. "We were asleep in our bed in Bellingham, and the phone woke us up. My wife keeps saying that she half expects to wake up again and realize none of this has been real." He sighed and pushed his empty glass across the bar. "I should get back, or my wife will start nagging at me again."

I studied his back as he exited the bar. The whole interaction had been difficult to read. His voice had never cracked with emotion, even when he said he was in town for his daughter's body. But some people kept those things close to their chest. Maybe he wasn't an emotive guy. I chewed on my lip. He could also be in shock. Or, worse, Bellingham was close enough to Point Pleasant that he could have come to town, murdered his daughter, and been home in time to be with his wife for the call. Either way, the interaction hadn't been as helpful as I had hoped. No questions had been answered, and no new questions had been introduced. Grumbling, I stalked out of the bar and walked the two blocks back to my car.

As I drove to my office, I kept the notebook with the list of suspect names open next to me on the passenger seat. *If I can't get anywhere with David, maybe I can get somewhere with Cyrus.* For the past three days, he had been holding morning prayer vigils in front of Abby's bistro. I didn't have time for a second stop, and he would probably be gone for the day already, but it was likely that he would be there again tomorrow. I would have to set my alarm for a few minutes early to make sure I caught him.

CHAPTER 7

My bad luck followed me for the rest of the day. A claim that had been reported as a sump pump failure in the crawl space turned out to be a sewage backup from the septic system instead. The next inspection was for a kitchen fire, which had happened at a hoarder's house. By the end of the day, I was on to my third change of clothes and seriously considering how difficult it would be to add a shower in my office.

I ducked out of work early, a perk of being self-employed. The entire ride home, Charlie stood with his paws braced on the armrest of the door, his nose pressed against the small opening in the window that I had left open a crack. I had spritzed some lemon linen spray on the bag of dirty clothes to make the drive home bearable, and he was displeased. Citrus was not his favorite scent.

When we got home, Charlie darted ahead of me, out of the car, and sprinted up the steps to the front door. I let him into the house, and he stared pointedly between me and the door that led to the mudroom in the kitchen. I chuckled and shuffled through the house to start a load of laundry and then take a shower before the Retirees arrived to build the model of Meredith Walker's house.

I had only been out of the shower for ten minutes when Betty's truck came to a stop in my driveway. The Retirees piled out of the truck. I put on a kettle for some tea and watched them through the kitchen window as they unpacked a couple small boxes from the back seat. I met them at the front door to let them in. They were still mid conversation as they filed into my house.

Betty shuffled past me first, the largest of the three boxes in her hands. "It doesn't have to be perfect—"

"It is the intention that matters—" Agnes cut in.

Sarah took up the rear. She clutched the smallest of the boxes against her chest, with a paper bag dangling from her other hand. "Normally I would agree, but the more accurate—"

Betty dropped her box on the kitchen counter. "We don't even know what's in the other rooms, though."

"—the model, the stronger the connection." Sarah continued as if Betty hadn't spoken.

My head swiveled between them as they continued arguing about intention over accuracy. "What is going on?"

"Sarah wants to make furniture for the model"—Betty gestured wildly—"and I don't think it's necessary. We know what our intentions are."

"Intentions are great, but there is sufficient evidence that a better focus leads to better results." Sarah crossed her arms over her chest.

Agnes flopped into a chair at the dining room table. "Sarah has a point."

Betty spun toward Agnes, her mouth gaping open. "You're supposed to be on my side."

Agnes held her hands up. "I'm on no one's side. I just want it to work."

"Okay." I took a seat opposite Agnes. "Could someone explain to me, like I'm a child, why we would or would not need furniture in the model?"

They all started talking at once.

I held up my hands, my index fingers pointed upward. "Wait! One at a time, please."

They glowered at each other and fell silent.

I motioned toward Agnes. "Since you're the one in the middle, you explain it to me."

"All right. You remember our explanation of sympathetic magic?" she asked.

I nodded.

"Well, there are two schools of thought when it comes to sympathetic magic. Not everyone"—she stared pointedly at Sarah—"is a talented artist. But being good at art isn't a prerequisite to being good at sympathetic magic."

"But it helps," Sarah grumbled under her breath.

Agnes pinched the bridge of her nose. "But it helps. Some argue the intention of the connection matters most, while others argue it is the accuracy... and to be honest, the truth is somewhere in the middle. It's easier to focus your intention on something accurate."

"Okay. So furniture?" I looked between the three women.

"When I picture Meredith's house"—Sarah held my gaze —"I picture the living room with the love seat and gramophone. I think our focus will be better if the model has those items."

"And I think it's an unnecessary waste of time. We know what the house looks like. We just need the model to focus on. Little pieces of toy furniture add nothing to that focus," Betty said.

"For you." Sarah shot a glare at Betty.

I closed my eyes and pictured the house. We weren't inside long before we found the markings left by the Wardens of the West, but Sarah was right. When I envisioned the interior, I saw the furniture. I also saw the ghastly woman at the top of the stairs who wailed and flew down them toward me. I shuddered at the image of her face. Her bright-green eyes had been eerie. "Do we have the materials to make the furniture?"

"Yes," Agnes piped in.

"And do we have time to make it before the next full moon?" I asked. Sarah could only use her magic during the full moon, and we needed all the magical juice we could get to make sure the divination spell worked.

"It's questionable. Have you ever built a dollhouse before? I sure haven't. Why risk adding to the list of things we've got to do?" Betty crossed her arms.

"You're not the one who's going to have to focus on the spell." Sarah pointed at me. "She is."

I swallowed. Divination was my strong suit. Intellectually, I knew that either Grace or I would be the one casting the spell, but hearing it said out loud made it more real. "Have you built a dollhouse?" I asked Sarah.

"Once." Sarah winced. "Sort of. I helped."

"I could use all the help I can get." I slumped into my seat. "Maybe we could build them second."

"We could have more dollhouse-building sessions," Agnes said.

"It will take time away from other witches' school lessons. Lessons Grace needs to get a handle on her abilities." Betty took a seat at the table and unpacked the boxes. "And I have been enjoying feeling like a useful witch for once."

"You are a useful witch." I put my hand over hers and squeezed. "I don't know what I would have done without you. But I don't want to mess this up. So... I think we should make the furniture too."

"All right. I'll just have to figure out a way to turn this into more of a lesson so we aren't skipping the classes we've promised to teach." Betty wiped at her eyes and then continued unpacking the box. "Anyway, where's Grace?"

I glanced out into the driveway. Her car was still gone. "I think she's still on one of her nature walks."

Betty nodded and finished unpacking. As she sorted through the items, the Retirees began talking again. They had a habit of talking over each other but somehow still being able to understand and carry on a conversation. I could only make out a little as they discussed turning the building of the model into a witch's lesson. I only half listened as I pulled out my laptop and opened my estimating software. It was useful for diagramming houses. I had spent the last few days poring through home listings from the same street as Meredith Walker's house to cobble together a floor plan. I flipped the screen and showed it to them.

"That looks great, Dani." Agnes pulled out a square piece of plywood about two feet long by two feet wide. "We should draw the basic shape here and then build it up in layers."

We got to work, first sketching it out and then gluing small wooden blocks down in all the corners. We had placed the last block when headlights filled the living room window. I glanced outside again. Grace was home. She trudged up the driveway toward us.

"We're in here," I yelled from my seat in the kitchen.

Grace poked her head around the doorframe. She looked exhausted. Her eyes were bloodshot, with bags under them. Her hair was in disarray. "I forgot it was model-building time." Grace glanced at her watch. "I've double-booked myself."

I picked up my notepad. "Don't worry. I'm taking notes."

Grace nodded and inched farther into the room. Her eyes focused on the model we had built. "It looks good so far. What are you going to do for the second floor?"

I showed her my diagram while the Retirees continued to work. "Still figuring it out, but it should look something like this."

She shook her head. "You're missing a door."

I looked between her and the screen. All of my sleuthing online indicated this was the right setup. It was the standard for the houses on that street, but I hadn't been upstairs long enough to remember the layout fully.

"There was a third door on the right." She tapped my screen. "It was thinner than the others. Maybe a linen closet?"

"Are you sure?" I asked.

Grace nodded and tapped the screen again. "It was right there."

I frowned and turned the screen around. Grace had been upstairs with me. I hadn't had time to count the doors. She might be remembering it better. My memory of the space had been overshadowed by Sarah screaming downstairs when she found out that the Wardens of the West had marked the building. I added in the door. Maybe there had been a linen closet.

Grace yawned and looked at the clock over the oven. "I've got to go. I promised Dad I would call him today. It's his birthday next week, and he's taking off tomorrow to go to the cabin in the woods."

Ed, my ex-husband, had always been a fan of his annual camping trips. His birthday was the first of the year.

I gave Grace a quick hug before she retreated from the room. I heard footsteps on the stairs, followed by her bedroom door opening and closing.

"Is she doing okay?" Betty asked.

I shook my head. "She's still barely sleeping."

"It must be getting even worse," Sarah said.

"I don't know, honestly." I pursed my lips. Grace's midnight screams were less frequent, but that didn't mean she was sleeping any better. It could mean she was sleeping even less than before. But she also insisted that her nature walks were helping calm her mind. I glanced down at Charlie and held his gaze. I let my concern for Grace flow through our connection. He nodded and trotted out of the room to go check on her. "She hasn't said anything."

"She might not, if it's gotten really bad." Betty patted my hand. "She's a lot like you. And you have a habit of keeping things to yourself to protect others."

I chuckled. It wasn't an amused chuckle but an acceptance of the truth. I was bad about letting people in, but it was something I was working on. Grace had helped me a lot. She told me over and over that keeping secrets from the ones you love helps no one. Secrets were something I still struggled with. I chewed on my lip as Chris came to mind. I was keeping Abby's visit from him. But if I told him and he kept it a secret and Bob found out, it would be disastrous for his career. I didn't want to be the one responsible for ending his dreams. I wasn't ready to tell him about Abby, and I wasn't ready to tell him I was a witch either.

I mentally checked in on Charlie. I could sense him sitting outside Grace's door. He batted at it again and meowed. The door didn't open.

Grace was hiding something, but it could be something as innocuous as her not wanting me to see her happy to talk to her dad. I mentally called Charlie back down the stairs and continued working on the model. The Retirees and I continued to chat as we worked, and by the end of the session, all the walls on the first floor were up, and Sarah had made a replica of the dining room furniture. The model was coming together, and soon we could use it to look back in time and witness how the curse began.

CHAPTER 8

I tossed and turned all night. No matter how hard I tried, I couldn't get thoughts of Abby out of my head. I climbed out of bed early, showered, and headed into town to bump into Cyrus at the morning prayer vigil for Emma. I slowed as I approached the intersection that led to Eats and Treats. There was a large group of people milling about outside. I tightened my grip on my steering wheel as I found a place to park. I only had one shot at this, and I hoped it would be more productive than my conversation with David.

Downtown was busy. The two-block walk passed in a blur as I tried to figure out how to start the conversation. My stride faltered as I got closer. A small memorial had been built in front of the boarded-up windows. On one side was Cyrus and his followers, and on the other was David, Sophia, and Robert. There was tension in the air as they competed in their prayers.

I still wasn't sure how to proceed as I joined the group. I stood halfway between them and studied the memorial. Emma stared out at me from her photo. She was young, maybe nineteen, with shoulder-length blond hair tied back in a ponytail. Her blue eyes were clear, and there was an innocent naivety in them. She had trusted whoever took that photo implicitly.

I sidled up next to Cyrus and stared down at the photo. I cleared my throat and bowed my head. "Did you know her?" I asked.

Cyrus nodded. "I gave her a safe place to land when she needed it."

"Oh?" I left the question short and open-ended. It was probing enough to get a response but open enough that the listener would feel almost compelled to overexplain.

"Yes." Cyrus glanced over at David and raised his voice. "Emma fled an abusive situation at home. She was finally coming into herself. Really coming out of her shell. I was so proud of the progress she had made."

David stiffened. Out of the corner of my eye, I could see him clenching his fists as his wife tried to whisper calming words into his ear. I ducked my head and turned away so he wouldn't see my face clearly. "Do you know why she would have come here? Point Pleasant is a little out of the way, isn't it?"

"I don't know." Cyrus raised his voice again so it carried down the block. "I suspect someone close to her had something to do with it. She always wanted to see the best in people, even when they *didn't* deserve it."

I glanced at David. He was shaking with rage. The vein in his forehead throbbed. His wife was wrapped around his arm, pleading with him. Her voice was so low, I couldn't make out the words. Cyrus was goading him on.

"I, for one"—Cyrus turned toward David—"plan to pray outside this establishment every day until her killer is brought to justice."

I gritted my teeth. *Is Cyrus egging David on because he thinks he's guilty or because he enjoys the chaos?* There was something about the smugness in Cyrus's eyes that made it feel more like he enjoyed the chaos. I cleared my throat again. "Do you know Abby?"

His eyes flicked to my face, and his smug expression wavered. He glanced back at his small congregation. "We really should start with our morning prayer. We're going to pass a candle around. Will you join us?"

"Of course." I stepped closer to Cyrus. My heart raced at the idea of touching something right after he had. It would be helpful to get a read on his emotional state.

Cyrus grabbed a candle from a bag at his side and lit it. He bowed his head over the candle and prayed. "Emma, I pray that you found the peace that you were looking for."

I held out my hand to accept the candle, but a girl stepped between us and intercepted it. My heart sank. It was the girl from the diner. The sides of her head had recently been re-shaved.

She added her prayer to the mix. "Emma, you welcomed me with open arms when I first arrived. When I was scared and new to living on the streets, you comforted me when no one else did. You were a good person. I pray your killer is found." She handed me the candle.

I followed suit and bowed my head. "Emma, I pray your killer is brought to justice." I handed the candle off to the next person.

The prayer circle continued like that. Each person began with her name and added a prayer. The candle ended in Cyrus's hands.

"Did you know Emma well?" I asked the girl next to me.

She held her finger to her lips as Cyrus added the candle to the memorial. It was the fourth one. He stood staring down at her face in silence. I glanced around the gathered group. Even David was silent. Everyone stood quietly, remembering her. After almost a full minute, Cyrus turned back to the group.

"It is time to get going. Lunch for the homeless isn't going to cook itself." He strode forward and looped his arm around the girl next to me. He turned her away before she could say anything further, and his congregation walked away down the street.

I sighed with frustration. The entire conversation had been performative. I glanced over at David. His wife, Sophia, and Victoria's father, Robert, stood clustered around him. My gaze landed on Robert, who I presumed was still looking for his missing daughter. *He might know something.* I took a step toward him. "Did you know Emma?"

"You again." David stepped in front of me. "What are you doing here?"

I stepped back and held my hands out to my sides to ease the tension. "I'm just… curious."

His anger flared. "You really are morbid, you know that?"

"I'm friends with Abby," I said.

"Abby?" David took another step forward and straightened to his full height so he could loom over me. "If you know where she is, you should tell me. Emma deserves better than this."

I fought the urge to shrink into myself. Facing down a large man wasn't something I ever thought I would get used to.

"David," Sophia said, "this is a small town. Leave the locals be."

Sophia stepped in close and put her hand tentatively on his shoulder. David stiffened under her fingers. He shrugged her off and turned away from me. He strode to the memorial and crouched down in front of it. Robert joined him, and Sophia hovered over the pair of them.

They prayed silently over Emma's photo before standing and walking down the street without another word. I studied their backs as they left. It had been another useless interaction. The conversation had been too public. Cyrus had been more focused on riling up David than providing information. All he had done was add to my suspicions that David had been an abusive father. But that didn't mean he killed his daughter. It just kept him high on my suspect list.

I knelt in front of the memorial and reached out to touch the candle. I gasped as the sensation of nothing filled me. It was stronger than it had been when I first encountered it, almost as if all the emotion had just been stripped from it. There was a rawness to the nothing. I closed my eyes and replayed the interaction in my head. There had been a lingering sadness when the girl handed me the candle. And then Cyrus took it… but I lost sight of the candle when David and Robert knelt in front of it. Any of three men could be possible.

I rocked back on my heels and pulled out my notebook. As I crouched there, I crossed off Sophia's name. It had to be one of those three men. And Cyrus, the only one I knew for a fact had touched the candle, was now at the top of my list.

CHAPTER 9

I spent the rest of my day replaying the events of the morning, shifting through each word, each look and motion, trying to find a thread to pull. All three of my suspects knew what I looked like, so my next attempt at an interview had to be different. I contemplated attempting the glamor spell that let me look like someone else but quickly dismissed the idea. Last time I had cast the spell, it took all of my focus to keep it up. I wouldn't have the mental capacity to pay attention to the details and hold the spell simultaneously. It wouldn't do me much good to have a slapdash conversation.

I was going through the motions of a roof inspection, marking wind-damaged shingles, when my phone rang in my pocket. The hairs on my arms stood up at the sound. I froze mid-motion and focused on the sensation. Normally I wouldn't answer the phone on the roof, but the hairs stayed up, despite the warming weather. I fished my phone out of my pocket and answered.

"This is Nora Niccols calling you back," a woman said. There were muffled voices in the background, like she was in an office.

"Hi." I wracked my brain to remember who Nora was. *The*

social worker? I sat down to force myself to stay still. "Thank you for calling me back. I had some questions about a community outreach program you're working on. I was wondering if we could meet in person to chat."

Papers shuffled in the background. "My schedule is pretty full already this week. I don't think I could squeeze you in until next Thursday. I'm available between two and four p.m. Does that work for you?"

My heart sank. Next Thursday was too long. Abby needed me now. I swallowed and took a risk. "I'm not sure it can wait that long. Sorry." I fumbled, trying to think of a name, and went with Robert's daughter. "I... I am not sure how to ask this, but is Victoria safe with Cyrus?"

"Is who safe with Cyrus?" There was a hesitancy in her voice.

"My daughter's friend. I just found out she was staying at some sort of halfway house. It's just... you hear horror stories about places like that. I'm sure most of them are fine. But I worry. My daughter thinks she can convince her friend to either go home or move in with us, and I didn't know if I should encourage that or not. Is Victoria safe with Cyrus Drake?"

Silence greeted me. I held my breath, waiting for her to respond. She hadn't hung up, so I pressed one last time. "Is he a good man?"

"I don't know," Nora mumbled. There was a strange shuffling sound on the other end, like she was holding the phone to her chest. It sounded like a door opened and closed, and then she was back. "I can't go into any specifics, you understand?"

I nodded and then croaked out a "yes."

"I just found out I'm not the only social worker who has placed kids in his care. I'm sure there is a legitimate reason he wouldn't have mentioned them to me, but... I honestly don't know how many there are. Every kid, especially at-risk kids like these, takes time and resources. There are caps for a reason. There are usually no more than six per house, and... I just... What if he doesn't have time to take care of them all?" She half squeaked as she asked the last question.

"Have you seen—"

"Until it's sorted, it might be a good idea to have your daughter encourage her friend to move someplace else that is safe. I've got to go. I shouldn't have told you that much."

The line clicked. I stared at my phone. Nora had been spooked. *Why would Cyrus hide how many kids are in his care?* I mulled it over as I finished my roof inspection.

On my way home, I stopped by the Bizzy Bean. The doors were closed, and the lights were out. I peered at a note on the door stating they had to close early but would be open at their usual time in the morning. I pulled out my phone and texted Heather.

> **DANI:**
> Everything all right? I saw the cafe was closed.

> **HEATHER:**
> Yes. Dealing with laundry at the B&B. It's never-ending.

> **DANI:**
> You up for company?

> **HEATHER:**
> Always. Especially if you know how to fold a fitted sheet.

I chuckled. Luckily, it was something my gran had taught me. I got out of the car and walked around the block to the back entrance. The laundry room was off the mudroom, which was connected to the courtyard in the back. The B and B overlooked the courtyard. Iris had planted flowers along the perimeter, with small cutouts for benches every fifteen feet. In the center was a giant maple tree that guests would frequently gather under in the summer. I found Heather in the walk-in linen closet, struggling with a king-size sheet.

"Give it to me." I held out my hand for it.

Heather sighed and handed it over. There was a stack of sheets next to her that were in various states of folded. None were done well.

"You start by putting your fingers into the corners, like this." I quickly showed her how to fold a fitted sheet.

"You would think I would know this," Heather said, following my directions. "But by the time Mom had me, she was stuck in her ways and never asked for help. I'm drowning in responsibilities."

"Any word on when Ash will get his room renovated?" I asked.

"They started hanging drywall today. He asked for one more week." Heather grabbed the next sheet in the pile. "How's your investigation going?"

I shrugged.

"That well, huh?" She shook her head.

I gave her an update on my conversation with Cyrus and the social worker.

"Wow." Heather's jaw dropped. "Do you think that means other girls are in danger?"

"Maybe." I grabbed the last sheet. "Nora seemed pretty scared by the idea he had too many people in his care."

"You should tell Chris." Heather grabbed the sheets and put them away on their designated shelf before grabbing the next batch from the dryer.

"It's not his jurisdiction," I said.

"True, but that doesn't mean he wouldn't know who to loop in."

I nodded and pulled out my phone.

> **DANI:**
> I had an interesting conversation with a social worker today about Cyrus.
>
> Apparently, he has more than one putting kids with him. There might be a concern that he has too many kids in his care to effectively take care of.

Dots appeared and disappeared as Chris typed. I stared at my phone, holding my breath until his message finally appeared.

> **CHRIS:**
> I'll look into it.

I grabbed the sheet from the pile. *What now? Do I go to a halfway house? Do I try to locate Robert for a one-on-one?*

Heather stared at me. I blinked as I realized I had been standing there, sheet in hand, staring blankly at it while I ruminated on the problem.

"Are you going to tell me what else is on your mind?" she asked.

I dropped the sheet and hopped up onto the counter. I slouched, my fingers digging into the wood beneath me. "It's bothering me that I can't pick up an emotional residue on some things. I found another object. A candle. And it was like hitting a wall. I don't know why I can't pick something up. Is it magic? Are there wizards? I didn't see any of the guys do anything to the candle other than touch it. And"—a fear that had been forming in the back of my mind tumbled out— "what if I can't sense it because I'm not strong enough?"

Heather pulled me into a hug. "Maybe you're not."

I gaped at her. "How is that supposed to make me feel better?"

"It's not." Heather leaned back and studied my face. "You

told me looking backward isn't what you're best at. But you know who is? Grace. Maybe you should ask her for help."

"I couldn't—"

"Why not?"

"She's dealing with enough already." I shifted on the counter. "What if she sees something awful and can't pull back?"

"She's not a kid anymore. Well, not a kid kid. You know what I mean. She's old enough to make that decision on her own. You should tell her what the problem is, and if she wants to help, she will."

"You know she's going to say yes." I crossed my arms.

"I do." Heather pointed at me. "And you know she will be mad if you keep her out of something important in a misguided attempt to protect her."

"It's not—"

"She can help you."

There was truth to her words. Grace was much better at looking into the past than I was. Not asking was pure motherly instinct. And Grace would be furious if she found out. *Secrets help no one* was her new mantra.

I hung my head. "Fine, I'll ask."

CHAPTER 10

I finished helping Heather fold the sheets, and then she ushered me out before I lost my nerve. I drove straight back home. Grace's car was outside our home when I arrived. I stared at it, my stomach churning. As I stood from the car, I wobbled as all my muscles quivered. I had never asked Grace for help like this before. I didn't know if I was more scared of her saying yes or saying no. Either way, it had the possibility of being awful. *I promised Heather I would do it. She's right. Grace will be upset if I don't. Just... walk in there. I can do this.*

I stood there for another minute before my internal pep talk was successful. Finally, I squared my shoulders and strode up the steps to the front door.

Grace was in the kitchen making dinner. She was sautéing onions. The scent of meat roasting in the oven and onions sizzling on the cooktop made my mouth water. She glanced over her shoulder as I came in. "You hungry?"

I nodded weakly.

"I'm making spaghetti and meatballs." Grace turned back to the stove and added a can of diced tomatoes to her onion mix. "I found the recipe on YouTube. It will be done in about fifteen minutes. I hope you don't mind me experimenting some."

"It smells delicious." I took a seat at the kitchen counter and watched her work. "When you have a minute, we need to talk."

Grace froze for a heartbeat. She hunched her shoulders and peered at me out of the corner of her eye. "About?"

"I…" I floundered. I stared down at my hands and picked at my cuticles as I spoke. My words came out as a jumble of words. "Abby asked me to investigate the murder at her bistro. I'm trying to. But when I went inside, I couldn't get a read on something. It was weird, like no one had touched it before. And I know someone has, and I thought maybe because you're better at psychometry that you might be able to pick something up that I missed."

Grace dropped her spoon into the pan and turned toward me. "What are you talking about? Could you say that again?"

"I found something that has no emotional residue."

"Before that."

"Abby asked me to help investigate a murder?"

"How long ago?" she asked.

"A couple days." I winced at her expression.

"Okay." Grace crossed her arms over her chest and glowered at me. "Putting that aside for now, what do you mean, no emotional residue? Everything has an emotional residue."

"This doesn't," I said.

"Like it's very faint?"

"No." I explained the sensation I'd felt. Her eyes got wider the longer I spoke.

She whistled. "Okay, I'll help. Or try to. If it really doesn't have an emotional residue, I'm not sure I'll be much use."

"It doesn't hurt to try," I said.

Grace nodded and turned back to her marinara sauce. It was bubbling slowly. She fished the spoon out and slowly stirred it. "After dinner."

My stomach rumbled. If we had to cast any spells, it would be a good idea to eat ahead of time. Magic exhausted me faster than an intense workout.

While we ate, we came up with a game plan. I would start by showing her the spots where I had felt nothing and then go into the alley behind the bistro. Grace would keep watch while I used the obsidian mirror to purposefully activate my Sight and get a vision of the night Emma was murdered.

Satisfied with our plan, I packed up the notebooks and the obsidian mirror as well as a few herbs, like lavender and rosemary, that helped with clarity and vision. As I packed, I joked that one of these days I would build myself a witches' kit, just like I had an inspection kit for my day job as a claims adjuster.

We drove in silence. I led her to the memorial and pointed out the candle I had touched earlier that day. Grace knelt beside it, pulled off her glove, and ran her fingers down its length. She closed her eyes and exhaled sharply.

"What do you feel?" I asked.

"Shock?" she whispered. "I think I'm feeling what you felt earlier."

I groaned. Of course she would feel my shock. It's common for newer emotions to overwrite an older one unless the older one was more intense. Nothing was nothing. It wouldn't take much to overwrite it.

Grace looked up and down the street. After the last of the dinner rush drifted out at eight p.m., downtown quickly emptied. By nine, the streets were deserted. All the neighboring businesses had closed for the night. "Maybe there's something inside?"

"We shouldn't." I shifted my weight between my feet. "As a responsible parent, I shouldn't be teaching you breaking and entering."

Grace snorted. "Was the scene cleared by the sheriff's office?"

"Yes."

"And Abby asked you for help?" Grace stood and stared at me.

I sighed. "Yes."

"It's not breaking and entering if we have permission."

"Fine." I pursed my lips. "You have a point."

She grinned. "Excellent. Now let's go inside."

Grace used her psychometry powers to figure out the combination to the lock. It only took her two tries to get the right number order. She held the door open for me, and I darted inside. She stepped in after me and closed the door behind us.

I pulled out my phone and used it as a flashlight to illuminate the space. Grace whistled as the destruction became visible. The room was as I last saw it. Contents strewn everywhere, with broken glass littering the floor.

"Someone really did a number on this place." Glass crunched under her feet as she moved deeper into the room.

"I was thinking we could start with the bins. It looks like someone pulled them out and dropped everything on the floor. It's likely the killer touched them."

Grace nodded and moved over to where the plastic bins that had housed the cutlery lay discarded in the corner. She reached out and touched the first container. "Shock." She moved on to the second one. "A bit of anger." As her hand landed on the third bin, she gasped. Her fingers splayed out across it as her whole body shook. "Nothing."

"You found it?" I scrambled forward and knelt down by her side. "It's odd, isn't it?"

"Yes," she croaked. She licked her lips and held her free hand out toward me. "It's almost like something's stopping me from reading it. Take my glove off. Maybe if we join hands, we can push through the barrier."

I grabbed her glove and gently removed it. Tentatively, I reached out and held her hand. She groaned at the contact. I steadied my breathing and focused my will into her palm. I visualized it as a thread going from me to her and through her into the object. Motes of white light swirled between us. She exhaled, and her green sparkles, with the occasional purple one, joined the mix.

Nothing. The same sensation she felt swarmed over me as the lights danced between us. The lack of anything was so jarring, it almost knocked me over. I closed my eyes and continued to visualize the thread. I forced more of my will into it. More motes of light flew out of me and swirled with the sparkles that flowed out of Grace at a rapid pace.

We hit the same wall again. There was an absence. I could feel the edges of it in my mind.

"Do you think another witch is involved?" Grace asked.

"I don't know." I gripped her hand as we pushed mentally against the void again. "Based on the height of whoever broke in, combined with who could have touched the candle last, I think we're looking at a guy. Do you think wizards exist?"

"I don't see why not." Grace shifted on her heels. "Why don't we try that trick Agnes taught us? If there's a spell on it, we might be able to see it."

Without moving her hand, we slowly shifted around the container until it was between us. I relaxed my gaze until it went out of focus and then slowly refocused on it. *Show me what's hidden.* I repeated the thought as a mantra as the plastic tote resettled in front of me.

There was a faint glow. So faint, it was hard to make out. I leaned closer, forcing my eyes to stay relaxed as I studied it. There were markings that appeared to be faded.

"Could you hand me my notebook?" I asked.

Carefully balancing on one foot, she widened her stance until she could reach my bag a few feet away with her foot. She snagged the handle with the tip of her shoe and pulled it closer while her other hand stayed flat on the surface of the plastic. Once it was in reach, I grabbed my notepad from the front pocket.

My legs shook under me as I continued to hold my deep squat. With one hand, I fumbled with the pad of paper and pen as I drew, careful to keep my other still clasped in Grace's hand. I copied the symbols as best I could before my legs gave out and I tumbled to the ground. I lost my connection to Grace, and the light of the magic winked out.

I sat on the floor, my legs still shaking. In the dim light coming in through the few windows that weren't boarded up, I could make out the rough shape of Grace sitting a few feet away. Her breathing was shallow but even as she hugged her knees to her chest.

"Are you okay?" I asked.

She cleared her throat. "Yes."

I crawled over to the bag of supplies we had brought with us and shoved the notepad back inside.

"Feeling nothing is the strangest sensation," Grace said. "On the one hand, it felt wrong because of how used I've become to feeling something, always. On the other, it was... freeing. Almost like floating in a deprivation tank. You know the ones where you're floating in saltwater, and you can't see, hear, or really feel anything?"

"That sounds like a nice change of pace." I crouched next to the bag and unpacked the first notebook I had ever received as well as an obsidian mirror and a clip-on reading light.

Grace was silent behind me for a few seconds before she responded. "I thought it would be. I've yearned for a time when I can go back to feeling nothing. But it was so... sharp in its edges. If that makes any sense. It was like touching dry ice. It was absolute silence. There was no background noise. It almost hurt how nothing it was."

I tiptoed back over to her, careful to avoid the bigger pieces of detritus scattered across the floor. The way her head hung forward, her chin resting against her knees, told me how exhausted she was. "I can cast the next spell if you're not feeling up to it." I said.

Grace pulled her legs tighter against her chest. "I just need a few more minutes."

I studied her back. She was incredibly strong-willed, but I couldn't put her through something that might hurt her. Not a second time. I flipped the book open to the right page, clipped a reading light to the notebook, and prepared myself for the next step in our plan—purposefully activating my Sight. The plan had been to do this in the alleyway, but I didn't want to make Grace move.

"I'm going to try it first." Without giving her time to respond, I raised the obsidian mirror up to eye level and launched into the spell. With one eye, I read the words of the spell, and with the other, I focused on the polished black stone. White motes of light floated out of my mouth and swirled around the room. The lights danced between the wreckage before flying back to me and settling into the mirror in my hand.

An image formed on the glass. It was the bistro as it used to be. All the broken items were whole. I turned in place slowly, moving the mirror up and down until I found a person. There was the top of a head, poking out from behind the dessert conveyor belt. I inched forward until I was in position to see behind the counter. Three girls huddled together, their eyes wide and fingers gripping each other's arms.

I recognized Emma from her memorial. She had her arms wrapped around another girl who was shaking with fear. Her hair was darker than Abby's, and she was much younger, but she had the same brown eyes as my friend. The resemblance was striking. I couldn't imagine her being anyone but Abby's sister. The third girl sat on the other side. She looked vaguely like the photos I had found of Victoria, except older. Her wavy dark-brown hair was in disarray, and she had a knuckle of her right hand shoved into her mouth to stay silent. Their eyes were trained on a spot not far from where I stood.

I took a faltering step back and spun in place to focus the mirror on the spot they were staring at. The glass fogged in my hand. I wiped at it, but nothing happened. The fog wasn't on the glass—it was in it. The fog obscured everything in that area from view. I gritted my teeth and padded slowly around the room, retraining the mirror on the same spot from multiple angles. It didn't help. Instead, the fog spread as whatever was hiding from me moved.

Nothing seeped into my hands. I gasped and fumbled with the mirror as it almost tumbled from my grasp. I dropped the spell, and the sensation dissipated.

"You see anything useful?" Grace asked. While I worked, she had risen shakily to her feet and retreated to the rear doorway. She stood, leaning against the doorjamb, with her arms wrapped around herself.

"I found the girls, but... the killer was like a cloud of fog." I shoved the mirror back into the bag.

"Maybe there's something helpful in the alley." She glanced over her shoulder.

I grabbed the bag from the floor and followed her outside. We moved together through the alleyway. I gripped her gloved hand. She squeezed back with just as much force. The alleyway walls were empty of signs or art. Above the back door of Abby's neighbor, there was a security camera pointing down.

"Do you think it would remember?" Grace asked.

"Maybe." I raised my hand to touch the camera. I had stuffed myself full of pasta less than an hour before, but I pushed myself hard in the bistro. With the way my hands were shaking, I wasn't sure if I had another spell in me. My fingers hovered over the glass lens. "You feeling up to casting another spell yet?"

Grace shook her head.

I dropped my hand and shuffled over, grabbed my bag, and dug through its contents. I had remembered to pack a lot of supplies but had neglected to include more food. It hadn't occurred to me that our first spell would exhaust us so much. More magic was out.

I glanced around the alley. The lights above the shop were on. I chewed on my lip. John Porter, who ran a glass-mural-making company, lived above his shop. He had been home the night of the incident, and it looked like he was home again now. Before I could talk myself out of it, I knocked on his door.

Another light turned on upstairs, followed by footsteps on the stairs. Not long after I had knocked, John pulled the back door open. He stood in the doorway, squinting out at me. He wore a craftsman's apron over a flannel shirt, jeans, and work boots. His hair was now more gray than red. He smiled, his entire face coming to life with warmth as he met my gaze. "Can I help you?"

"Hopefully." I stepped forward and offered my hand. "I don't know if we've formally met yet or not. I'm Dani."

He held my hand gently, despite his hands being rough and calloused. "It's a small town. Everyone knows who you are."

I gulped. *It would be a disaster if he formed his opinion based on what Bob said. Having the sheriff dislike me was really inconvenient sometimes.* I forced a smile onto my face. "Only good things, I hope."

"The best." He stepped backward into the foyer. "Would you like to come in for some tea? I expect you have questions about Abby."

I exhaled sharply and stifled a laugh. It was almost as if he had been expecting me. *Am I really that obvious?* I took a step inside, with Grace close behind on my heels. "That sounds lovely," I said.

He led us upstairs to his apartment. It was a large space but still somehow cramped. Art supplies and half-completed projects took up every spare inch. There was a small clear space in the kitchen where he had a round table barely big enough to fit four chairs around it.

He put on the kettle while he talked. "Abby has always been a great neighbor. Every night when she closes up, if she has some food left over she thinks I'll like, she'll walk it over. I forgot to eat once while working on a big project, and she's been worried about me ever since. She's a sweet kid, really."

"That sounds like the Abby I know." I took a seat at the table. Grace perched on one next to me, careful not to touch anything.

He grabbed mugs from the cupboard. They were irregularly shaped, and they shone under the light. "When I heard through the grapevine that she was a person of interest, I was tempted to go give Bob a piece of my mind. But I doubt that curmudgeon would listen."

"He is pretty stuck in his ways," I said.

Grace fiddled with the sleeves of her sweater and listened to our conversation, her head bowed to avoid attention.

The kettle whistled, and John poured the hot water into the mugs and handed them to us. The irregular shape was comfortable in my hand. It was like it had been made to be held.

"But I don't have much I can tell you. I wish it were different." He sipped his drink. "It was late. I was exhausted from working on a project all day. I had just put down my tools when I heard the ruckus. I looked outside but couldn't see much other than Abby running down the alleyway. These old bones don't move as fast as they used to. By the time I got downstairs, she was gone. The back door of her place was ajar. When I peeked inside and saw that it was trashed, I called the cops."

"Did you see anyone with her?" I asked.

"I didn't." He cocked his head to one side. "I was half asleep when I first saw her and didn't have my glasses on yet. But I could make out another person on the security camera."

My heart skipped a beat, and I inched forward in my chair. "Do you still have the footage?"

"Yeah." He gestured behind him. "I gave a copy to the police, but I still have the original."

"Would you mind if I watched it?"

"Don't see why not." He stood and retrieved his laptop. He pulled up the video and played it for me.

As he had described, it was dark out. The camera was facing down the alley, away from Abby's back door. Ten seconds in, Abby ran into view. There was another girl in front of her, half hidden from view by Abby's body. Abby wrapped her arms around the girl as they scurried down the alley. A second girl ran after them. At the end of the alley, Abby turned, her eyes wide, and stared back. She pushed both girls behind her before she stumbled back and out of view. Nothing else came into view.

"Could you play it again?"

He nodded. I pulled out my phone and recorded the scene.

"How long did the ruckus go on for?" I asked. Abby's place had been destroyed. It would have taken time to empty all those containers.

He shook his head. "I couldn't say. I had a deadline coming up, so I was working most of the night. I doubt I would have heard anything over my own hammering."

I thanked him for his time and finished the tea. He shared a few more stories about Abby and wished us a good night.

Grace shuffled after me to the car. We sat together in silence, staring at the dark bistro storefront. I pulled out the phone and replayed the video again. Abby was running away from something. But I couldn't see what. Or who.

"Do you think a ghost might be responsible?" Grace asked.

I shoved the phone back into my pocket. "I don't know, but at this point, I'm not ruling out any possibilities."

CHAPTER 11

"Rebecca, please, wake up!" Abby wailed. Her legs were sprawled out in front of her as she clutched her dead sister to her chest. She shook back and forth, tears streaming down her face.

Where am I?

I scurried toward her on all fours, trying to keep my head down. A chill breeze bit into my skin.

Is this a dream? I couldn't get my head to move. I had no control over my body. It was like I was watching a movie from behind someone else's eyes. *Okay, I'm dreaming. This is a prophetic dream. Pay attention to the details. Abby's alive. Her sister is dead. I'm a third person. Victoria?*

I slid to a stop next to Abby and glanced behind me. It was dark, but I could make out a wrecked black Toyota Prius. *No moonlight. But I'm definitely outside. Cloud cover, maybe?* The front end was crunched in, and the front windshield had a large spiderweb crack in the center. *Yellow paint? Were they in an accident?*

"We have to get out of here," I spoke in a woman's voice that I didn't recognize. *Definitely Victoria.*

"I can't just leave her," Abby sobbed.

I turned back and grabbed Abby by her arm. As my gaze slid back to her, I studied the ground as best I could. *Cement. No debris.* Abby was sitting in front of another wrecked vehicle. This one wasn't as bad. This one was a red SUV with a long, white streak down its side and ripped metal over the rear passenger door that reminded me of damage done by the lug nuts of a big rig in motion.

Two damaged cars? But they weren't in the same accident. Is this a salvage lot?

"I can't just leave her," Abby whimpered again.

Something crunched behind me. *A fourth person? Was that a footstep?* I half turned when pain shot through the side of my head.

I gasped as I sat up in bed. Cold sweat drenched my back. I scrambled to my feet and darted across the room to my purse to grab a notebook. I flipped to a blank page and jotted down everything I had seen. It was a cloudy night and someplace where beat-up cars were stored. My pen froze over that word. Stored. The hair on my arms was still up from the dream. My thoughts were foggy. But there was something about that word that was important.

I retreated to my bed and sat down hard as it clicked into place. Sinclair Auto Body. It was owned and operated by Keith Sinclair, Abby's father. She had gone home to her dad.

I threw on a pair of jeans and grabbed a sweater from the top drawer. I hopped down the stairs as I shoved my feet into tennis shoes. Within minutes of waking up, I was out the door and driving. It had been overcast all week, and according to the weather app on my phone would be for two more days. My visions of the future were always of something that was about to happen. The furthest out I had ever seen was a week. Which meant the attack on Abby was either happening tonight or sometime in the next two nights. I gripped the steering wheel until my knuckles turned white as

I drove through town at one in the morning. There was a small window of time, and I had to stop it.

Sinclair Auto Body sat on the outskirts of town. It was on a sprawling lot that had an eight-foot chain-link fence around it. Keith lived in a trailer at the back of the property. I parked and jumped out of the car. The gate was locked for the night, and a single bright bulb illuminated the lot. I cupped my hands around my eyes and peered inside. In the middle of the lot was the black Prius, and a few feet away was the red SUV from my dream. The cars were here. The sky was cloudy. My chest tightened, and I spun in place, searching the darkness for any sign of movement. Everything was quiet and still. A cold sensation settled into my gut, and I turned back to the gate.

There was no way to get up to Keith Sinclair's door to warn him. I darted back to my car and laid on the horn. I honked it five times before a light turned on in the trailer, and Keith stepped outside in his pajama bottoms. He wasn't tall, but he was broad and well-muscled. His salt-and-pepper hair was clipped short to his head. He held a wrench in one hand, and he stalked toward me with barely contained fury on his face. "Do you know what time it is? For Pete's sake, Dani, get off my property."

I ignored my fear response and ran to the gate. "Is Abby okay?"

He faltered, his expression going from rage to confusion. He swallowed and lowered the wrench. "How should I know? I haven't seen her in days."

"Please, I need to see her." I slipped my fingers through the chain link and pulled myself closer. "I have this horrible feeling. If you know where she is, I've got to know."

"She ain't here." Keith turned back to his trailer.

"I think someone's going to try to kill Rebecca."

He froze and peered at me over his shoulder. He wet his lips. "Like I said, she—"

"It's all right, Dad." Abby stepped out from the trailer. "I trust her."

Keith sagged and shuffled toward the gate. "If you do anything to hurt her…" He looked me up and down, distrust in his eyes, and let me in.

I nodded and stepped into the yard. I fought the urge to run to Abby. It wasn't like I could clearly explain why I was there at one in the morning. No one outside of my small inner circle knew I was a witch, or that witches existed. A bad dream wouldn't mean anything to them. I followed him back to the trailer, where Abby stood waiting, her arms wrapped around herself. She was backlit, which made her pixie cut look almost like a halo.

"What happened?" Abby asked.

"I can't explain it. Sometimes I get these feelings. When I woke up, I just knew," I said.

"That someone was going to kill my sister?"

I nodded.

Abby cocked her head to the side, nodded, and then stepped back into the trailer. "You might as well come inside."

The trailer was larger than expected. Keith had modified it to include a large bump-out on the other side, which turned the small two-and-a-half-room space into three. Peering out at me from behind a curtain was Abby's sister. I recognized her from my vision. She looked younger in person. She was maybe sixteen. Her brown eyes were so wide and expressive, it was hard not to internalize her fear when our eyes met.

"It's okay. You can come out," Abby said.

Abby's sister shuffled out from behind the curtain, with Victoria on her heels. Victoria had her long brown hair in a braid that went down to her hips.

"Who are you?" Victoria asked.

"My name's Dani." I held my hands out at my sides. "I'm here to help."

"I'm Victoria." She twisted her braid between her fingers. "Most people call me Vicky."

"Nice to meet you, Vicky." I turned my gaze to the other girl. "You must be Abby's sister. Rebecca, right?"

"Becca." She stared down at her feet.

Abby grabbed a folding chair from the corner and set it up next to the small card table in the middle of the room. There were already four chairs around it. She sat down and motioned for everyone else to sit.

"Okay." Abby perched on her seat, her shoulders back and her eyes trained on my face. "Someone is going to try to kill my sister. Do you know who?"

I shook my head.

She nodded. "If I had to guess, I would assume Cyrus."

"Is he the one who you ran away from at the bistro?"

"I think so." Abby's shoulders curled inward. She glanced at the other girls and glowered and straightened again. It looked like she was fighting her fear. "It was too dark. I couldn't see well. I can't say for certain, but... who else could it be?"

Becca and Victoria took seats on the opposite side of the table from me. They clung together, their hands intertwined and their eyes bouncing from me to Abby to the door.

"What were you doing there that night?" I asked.

Abby lowered her gaze. She grabbed her sister's hand and squeezed. "Becca called me. She asked if she could stay with me for a few days. I couldn't say no."

I turned my head toward Becca. "Why did you need a place to stay?"

Becca looked away from me and mumbled something under her breath. I leaned forward, trying to hear, and she scooted backward.

"She said that they had just escaped Cyrus and needed time to figure things out."

I inched backward to give the girls space. They were still in shock, and if I pushed, they might bolt.

"Why haven't you guys gone to the police?" I asked, softening my voice.

"I tried to convince them…" Abby sighed.

"Cyrus has friends everywhere. What if the cops didn't believe us? They would have taken us right back to him. They've done it before." Becca sounded a lot like Abby. They had a similar tone and inflection.

"It's only a matter of time before someone comes looking for you here." I held still as I spoke to avoid spooking them. "I have this horrible feeling, and my intuition is hardly ever wrong. I think you should come stay with me."

The room was silent after I spoke. The girls across from me were stock-still. Abby ran her fingers back and forth along the edge of the table, deep in thought.

Keith stood a few feet away, his shoulders rounded inward, and his oil-stained hands pressed on the counter behind him. "She's right."

Becca, Vicky, and Abby turned to him in unison, their eyes wide.

"The sheriff has already been by twice. Next time might actually be with a warrant. And Cyrus ain't no dummy. He probably suspects you are all here." Keith shuffled his feet. "They probably wouldn't expect you to be at some dame's place. I mean, from what I've heard she investigates everything, but housing you? I don't think it would occur to anyone."

Abby stood. "Then we should get packing."

CHAPTER 12

Abby and the girls didn't have much stuff with them. It only took five minutes for them to shove their measly belongings into a bag and pile into my car. Before we left, Keith made sure all our phones were charged and had his number in them, just in case. After I got them home and set them up in the daylight basement, I retreated to the dining room. Grace was asleep in her room. With all the trouble she had had sleeping since her powers manifested, I couldn't bring myself to wake her. Instead, I sat and wrote a note so she would know what was going on.

> Grace,
> Abby and her younger sister are staying with us for a while. They've brought a friend too. They seem like sweet kids, just very scared. I know it's not the best time, but they need a safe place to stay.
> If it gets to be too much, tell me and I'll try to figure something else out.
> I love you, and we'll get through this together.
> Mom

I was too wired to sleep, so instead I sat, drinking coffee and watching the time tick by until it was time to go to work. I left Charlie behind to watch over the girls. It wasn't perfect, but from a distance if I focused, I could still feel him and would know if everything was all right.

The streets heading into Point Pleasant were mostly deserted, with only a few early-morning commuters on the road. I always left a few minutes early to beat the morning rush. I glanced out my window as I rolled past the Bizzy Bean. Chris's car was parked out front. Being near him always comforted me. I pulled into a spot next to him and went inside.

Chris was waiting next to the large plexiglass cat enclosure for his drink. He was wearing his usual deputy uniform. He was due for a haircut. His normally close-cropped brown hair had reached the tips of his ears. Behind him, the kittens were batting at the glass to get his attention. He periodically looked down at them, a soft smile on his lips, and knocked on the glass with his heel. The kittens scattered, before regrouping and attacking the same spot on the glass, their little paws thumping against the enclosure behind him.

I sidled up to him and tapped him on his shoulder. He glanced down at me and raised his arm so I could slip in next to him. He rested his arm across my shoulders and kissed the top of my head.

"I wasn't expecting to see you this morning," he said.

"I saw your car and couldn't help myself. I had to come say hi." I snuggled into his side. "You hear anything back yet on Cyrus?"

"Yeah." He shifted his arm to see my face better. "They're still counting. The last number I heard was thirty-seven."

"Is that a lot?" I asked.

He nodded. "He only has one group home. They usually max out at six."

"Wow." I pursed my lips. "That's... wow."

"I was planning on telling you tonight on our date. Are we still on?"

I winced. With everything going on, I had forgotten about it. Abby and her sister were still in danger. And with magic involved, I couldn't count on the sheriff being able to solve this one without my help. *Should I tell him? I can't. It would put him in an awkward position.* "I'm swamped with work. Rain check?"

"Okay." He kissed the top of my head again. "This time next week, then?"

I pursed my lips. I hated postponing. Our dates were hard enough to schedule as it was, but I didn't know how long the investigation was going to take. "It's really hectic. I'll call you as soon as it clears up."

A look of disappointment flashed across his face.

"I'm sorry." I squeezed his hand. "I was really looking forward to it."

He smiled weakly and kissed the top of my head again. "It's okay. I'm used to scheduling issues. It would have been nice to have a distraction, you know?"

"Chris," Heather called from behind the counter. She was holding a to-go cup of coffee in her hand.

Chris slid his arm off my shoulder and stepped forward. I chewed on my lip as he grabbed his drink from Heather. Abby needed me to solve this sooner rather than later. I mentally reorganized my week to find time for the investigation. I didn't have any inspections scheduled for the morning. If I brought my work computer home with me, I could put together the estimates tonight after dinner. With my mind already on the case, I turned to leave.

"You headed out already?" Chris caught up to me and held open the door.

"No rest for the wicked." I stood on my tiptoes and kissed him lightly on his cheek. "I'll see you later."

I climbed into my car and pulled out my phone. I couldn't

think of a thread to pull on, so I had to find myself one. It wasn't a well-formed plan, but surveillance was my best shot at figuring something out. If Cyrus was really going to try to kill Abby's sister in the next two days, then maybe I could catch him doing something nefarious first. I doubted he would try something at the prayer vigil, so I had to catch him before or after it.

I opened the newspaper article that had a photo of Cyrus front and center. I had never tried to use my tracking spell on a person before, only on objects, but in theory, it worked the same way. With my phone in one hand and a map of western Washington in the other, I mumbled the words to the tracking spell. As the motes of light hit the screen of my phone, they spurted and died. *Did I cast it wrong?* I tried again, to no avail.

I dropped my phone in my lap and fumbled in my purse for the notebook with the tracking spell. I had the spell right. It just hadn't worked. I scanned through the notes my gran had written about the spell and groaned. In a footnote, it said the spell rarely worked on individuals—because their identities were too complex and always shifting—for the spell to latch onto. It provided examples on how to get visions of people from afar, also known as scrying, but even those said it worked better on a place than a person.

Slumping into my seat, I hit the steering wheel out of frustration. *How can I find him? Wait for his prayer vigil to start and follow him from there?* If Cyrus started the vigil at the same time every morning, it was still over two hours away. A lot could happen in two hours. I grabbed my phone and studied his photo. *Maybe he's wearing something I could find instead.* I zoomed in and panned over the image until I found something—a small pouch hanging from a leather strap around his neck. With a grin on my face, I pulled up his social media page and flipped from photo to photo. In each one, I could find the necklace.

With the map in one hand and my phone in the other, I zoomed in on the necklace and tried the spell again. This time, it worked. The motes of light flittered from my mouth to the phone and then onto the map. The lights clustered on the southern tip of Whidbey Island. My smile widened. Cyrus was in town.

Flipping to a map of Point Pleasant, I cast the tracking spell one last time. Cyrus was a few blocks away at the Slice of Life diner. I shoved the map back into my glove compartment and put my car into reverse. I drove to the diner and parked outside. Before heading inside, I texted Heather.

DANI:
We need to sit down for a proper update soon, but the short version is, I think Cyrus is responsible. He is at the Slice of Life diner right now. I'm going to follow him.

Don't worry. I'll take precautions.

After my last few investigations had turned violent, I had promised to keep Heather updated so she knew I was safe. I shoved my phone back into my pocket and exited the car.

The diner was busier than usual. It always had an early-morning rush, before most of the rest of the downtown businesses opened their doors, but now it was packed. Abby's bistro being closed for business had forced her usual morning crowd to find other establishments, and Willow's diner was tied for the best place to eat in Point Pleasant. Willow stood behind the counter, rapidly taking orders and calling them back to her line cooks in the kitchen.

My stomach growled at the scent of bacon. I scanned the room and found Cyrus sitting at the counter. I faltered as I got in line to place an order to go. He was sitting next to David Wilson. *What on earth are they doing together? I thought David hated Cyrus.*

As the line moved forward, I lowered my lashes until my

eyes were barely open and mumbled the words to the spell that would heighten my senses. The jeans I had put on that morning had a rough seam on the left inner thigh. Normally, it wasn't something I would notice. But with my senses heightened, it was hard to block out. The pain of the tiny stitches digging into my skin was sharp and insistent. *Note to self. When I buy more clothes, make sure I heighten my senses while wearing them before I leave the store.* I went through the motions of lowering my other senses back to normal, starting with my sense of touch.

I left my heightened hearing up. It was almost overwhelming. There were at least forty people in the diner, and half of them were talking. The clink of cutlery sounded like a hammer falling on concrete. I gritted my teeth and focused, trying to find Cyrus's voice in the mix.

The line in front of me moved at a quick pace. I followed the person in front of me as I narrowed down the voices to two.

"Don't believe me? See for yourself," Cyrus said. I watched him out of the corner of my eye as he stood, shoved his hands into his pockets, and strode out the door.

My stomach growled again. I could always cast the tracking spell again. After I had food in my stomach. I glanced over at David. He sat hunched over his plate. Next to him on the counter, at the place Cyrus had been sitting, was an envelope. David grabbed the envelope and shoved it into his pocket.

I swallowed. *Who do I follow now? Is this some sort of bribe?* I dropped my heightened senses spell as I stepped up to the counter to put in my order for a bacon, egg, and cheese breakfast sandwich to go.

I stared at David's back as he finished eating his breakfast. Before my order was called, he stood, tossed cash onto the counter, and walked out, his hands shoved deep into his pockets. I shifted from foot to foot impatiently until my order was called and then dashed out of the diner after him. When I got outside, he was already in his car and driving away down the block. I grabbed my phone and snapped a photo of his vehicle before he vanished out of view.

I climbed into my car and inhaled my breakfast sandwich. David was only a few minutes ahead. I couldn't imagine him leaving town yet, and I was willing to bet he was either headed to the bistro to attend another prayer vigil or back to his motel room. They were both in the same direction. I slowly drove past Madison Street and glanced down the block at the memorial for Emma. The sidewalk was empty of people, so I continued on to the motel where David and Sophia Wilson were staying. After fifteen minutes, I pulled up outside the motel. His car was parked outside his room. I drove around the block and found a space across the street to sit and wait. I texted Heather about the change of plans and put on an audiobook to help pass the time.

Despite having just eaten breakfast, my stomach was still rumbling. All the magic I had been throwing around the past few days had used up my stores of energy. I grabbed a protein bar from my bag and munched on it while I waited. They weren't my favorite, but I liked to think they were a healthy choice. At least the fake chocolate taste had improved over the years. While I waited, I periodically closed my eyes and focused on my connection to Charlie. All was well back at the house.

After forty-five minutes, the door to the Wilsons' room finally opened. Victoria's dad, Robert, stepped out first, followed by David and Sophia. Robert squeezed Sophia's shoulder and took a step back. He raised his hand awkwardly and turned to walk away. Sophia's makeup was blotchy, and her eyes were red. She clutched a tissue between her hands, which she used to blot tears. David's face was pale. He locked the motel room door behind him and shoved the key card into his back pocket.

I leaned forward and unrolled my window. The Wilsons didn't have any bags with them. I glanced at the clock on my dashboard. If they kept to the same schedule as they had the past few days, they were off to the prayer vigil. I wetted my lips. *Should I chance it?* David unlocked the car and held the door open for Sophia. She shuffled forward and collapsed onto her seat. He closed the door behind her and walked around the car to his side.

Follow them or snoop? I had a split second to decide. It was weird staring at David's bottom as he walked around the car. I whispered the words to the summoning spell and pictured a key card in my mind. Or at least what I assumed the key card would look like. Intent was what mattered. The motes of light sputtered as the image shifted in my head. I gritted my teeth and shoved as much of my will as I could into the words. The lights became brighter and flew between David and me. A second before he sat down, the key card slipped out of his pocket and slid across the ground toward me.

David shut his car door. The key card was still sliding across the ground as he drove away. I stared at it, continuing the spell until it reached my car. I opened the door and grabbed it off the pavement.

My hands shook as I picked it up. This was a risky move. *Too risky?* My eyes flicked around the parking lot. There wasn't anyone out and about, but that could change at any second. I didn't want anyone to see me, so I would make them see someone else.

I dug in my purse for the second journal I had received from my grandmother. With all four of the journals shoved in there, it was a tight fit, and I had to tug to get it out from the bottom. If I got another one, I would need to upgrade to a bigger bag.

I flipped the book open to the page that had the glamor spell. Wetting my lips, I stared at myself in my rearview mirror as I murmured the words to the spell. I didn't have a particular person in mind. I tried to picture a maid. My outfit changed first, from my sweater to a navy-blue uniform I had seen other maids wearing. My hair changed colors from almost black to an auburn color, and my steel-gray eyes shifted to brown. Last time I cast it, the spell took my full concentration. While I had improved a lot since then, it still took a lot out of me to hold it in place. I felt like I could hold it longer, but casting a second spell at the same time was still out of the question.

With my disguise as a maid in place, I slipped out of my car and strode across the parking lot to the Wilsons' room. I ducked my head so my face wouldn't be in view of any cameras. The glamor worked best on people. It was questionable if it would show up on film. I didn't want to risk it. I unlocked the door and ducked inside.

When the door closed behind me, the sounds of the street disappeared. The room had good soundproofing. I stood in front of the door, taking in my surroundings. There were two queen beds, a recliner next to a lamp, and a long table along one wall with a TV on top and a fridge and wooden chair under it. The room was clean. Both the beds were made, but the one in the back didn't have tucked corners.

I made a beeline to the rear bed and searched the nightstand next to it. There was a bible but nothing else in the drawers. I opened the closet. The Wilsons were the kind of people who unpacked at motel rooms. They had four changes of clothes hanging up and a folding laundry basket tucked into the corner. The basket was empty. I ran my hands over the clothes, quickly checking the pockets. They were empty.

If I were incriminating evidence, where would I be? I paced the room, my eyes darting from place to place. The safe was partially open. They hadn't paid to use it. I ran my fingers under the mattress. There was nothing hidden beneath it. I stopped in front of the long table. It had a binder of things to do in Point Pleasant and two drawers. I opened the one at the top and paused. Sitting alone in the drawer was a white envelope.

In large block letters, it had a name and address on it, but it had never been mailed. It was addressed to Sophia. My fingers hovered over the paper. I steadied my breathing and lowered my hand.

My throat thickened, and my heart became heavy in my chest. Tears formed at the corners of my eyes. I choked back a sob as I picked up the envelope. The grief and despair rolled off it in waves. It was hard to stand and still hold it. My hands shook as I flipped it over. The envelope wasn't sealed. I slid my fingers under the flap and froze again. Through one hand, I felt a grief so profound it was disorienting, and with the other, I felt absolutely nothing. My mouth went dry. I was certain the last person to touch this page was the killer.

I shook my head and pulled out the letter.

Mom,

I hope this letter finds you well. I'm sorry I didn't write sooner. You know me. I have a hard time with difficult words. It is somehow harder because life has been so fulfilling and busy that time just slips away. I know you must be worried about me, and I'm truly sorry for any distress I've caused you and Dad when I left.

I want to assure you that I am genuinely happy here. I've found a sense of purpose and belonging that I've never experienced before. Everyone here is like a family to me, and I feel more connected and loved than I ever have. I know you always tried your best, but I also know you could tell I didn't fully belong. It might be hard to understand, but being here has brought me a peace I've longed for.

I understand you and Dad have had your concerns about my decision to leave home. I've had my moments of doubt, too, but I've come to realize that this is where I'm meant to be. Cyrus is a wise and compassionate person who truly cares about every resident. He has guided me and helped me grow in ways I never thought possible.

Please don't worry about me. I'm safe, I'm happy, and I'm surrounded by people who support and care for me. I hope you can find it in your heart to trust my judgment and stop trying to bring me back home. I know it's hard, but I need you to believe in me and my choices.

I love you both so much and think about you every day. Please send my love to Dad and tell him I miss him too. I hope one day you can understand why I've chosen this path and find comfort in knowing that I'm content and at peace.

With all my love,

Emma

My hands shook as I laid the letter flat on the table. I took out my phone and snapped a picture before folding it gently and putting the letter back where I found it.

The tires of a car crunched against the concrete outside. I ducked in front of the bathroom mirror to make sure my illusion was still in place, quickly fixed my hair, and darted outside before anyone could find me in the room uninvited. I dropped David's key in the parking lot near where he parked and then ducked my head and scurried back to my car.

I stared at the photo of the letter. *Had it been opened when Cyrus gave it to David? Who touched it last?* The grief seemed to indicate Sophia had, but… when I got a letter from my gran after her passing, I had shoved it aside without reading it first. Grief can do strange things to a person. Any one of them could have been the last to touch it. To solve this one, I needed Becca or Vicky to talk.

CHAPTER 13

I had spent the rest of the day performing inspections and catching up on paperwork. Through pure force of will, I managed to get the estimates I needed written done before the end of business day. I didn't have to bring my computer home with me. Grace's car was gone when I pulled into the driveway. I parked and slumped into my seat with my eyes closed. I could have been on a date with Chris right now, but instead I was mentally preparing myself for questioning two traumatized girls. *How has this become my life? I wish I could ask Chris for help. He's better at questioning people than I am. But I promised Abby.* I hoped he would understand when the investigation was over.

"I'm home," I called out as I pushed the front door open. As I walked into the house, I relaxed my shoulders and forced a comforting expression onto my face.

I walked straight to the kitchen and peered into the fridge. It was half empty. I hadn't had a chance to go to the store yet this week, so most of the items were staples like ketchup, mustard, and milk. There was a head of cabbage, carrots, kielbasa sausage, and some potatoes that were forming sprouts on the counter. I grabbed the ingredients and started chopping.

"Your knife skills need work," Abby said from the door. "I can teach you a few tricks if you want. Or... since you're letting me stay, I can cook."

I put the knife down and retreated from the counter. "How about both?"

Abby took a hesitant step into the kitchen, her eyes trained on the window over the sink. I darted forward and closed the curtains. She exhaled and crossed the room to wash her hands. "How about I start by showing you the claw grip?"

"What's that?" I asked.

Abby picked up the knife and began chopping the carrots. "You curl your fingers into a claw shape and use your knuckles as a guide for the knife." She demonstrated. Her chops were quick and efficient. Within a few seconds, she was done with one carrot and moving on to the next.

I took a seat at the kitchen table and watched her work. Between chops, she glanced around, her eyes bouncing between me and the various doorways. Her shoulders were hunched. It looked like she was ready to bolt at any second. I held myself still, and slowed my breathing so I appeared at ease on the stool. One thing I had learned over the years handling claims was people had a tendency to meet you where you were. If you acted calm long enough, it eventually calmed them down as well. It was hard to stay anxious when talking to someone who clearly wasn't. Giving off an impression of calm did more good than telling someone to calm down ever could. The longer I sat there and patiently asked questions about food, the calmer Abby became. By the time Becca and Vicky emerged from the basement, with Charlie in tow, Abby was almost back to her normal self.

The girls lingered in the doorway before taking seats

across from me at the table. Charlie jumped up onto the chair next to me and headbutted my shoulder. He was letting me know they were okay.

"How was your day?" I asked, keeping my tone warm.

Vicky shrugged and hugged her arms to her body. Her fingers dug into her arms as she made herself as small as possible on the chair.

"Your daughter, Grace, let us watch your TV. I hope that's okay." Becca glanced past me to the living room.

"Of course." I scratched Charlie under his chin as I forced myself to stay relaxed. "If you want, I could also go rent some movies or grab a few books from the library."

"That would be lovely." Abby studied me and mirrored my body language as she moved on to the cabbage, slicing it into thick wedges. "Wouldn't it, Becca?"

Becca nodded, her eyes bouncing between Abby, me, and the doors.

"Any requests?" I asked.

"I like fantasy," Becca murmured.

I glanced between the girls and Abby. There was a tenseness in the air. Abby had picked up on my body language and was doing her best to emulate it, but it was hard when a murderer was still out there. The tenseness had a way of sneaking back into my shoulders. I rolled them back to loosen them. "How about food? I need to hit up the grocery store anyway. Any requests? Vicky, what's your favorite meal?"

Vicky dropped her hands to her lap. "Don't laugh, but I could really go for some fried chicken."

"That sounds delicious," I said.

"I miss bagels," Becca said. "I used to go to this place downtown that had jalapeno cheddar bagels with a smoked salmon topping. They were divine."

"How am I not surprised that you're also a foodie?" I chuckled and settled back in my chair. I kept my movements slow as I put a friendly smile onto my face. "The best meal I've ever eaten was made by your sister."

Abby ducked her head and continued chopping.

"What was it?" Becca asked.

"Japanese curry," I said. "She served it with chicken katsu and an egg that she had boiled in soy sauce. She was playing with Japanese food in honor of our cherry blossom festival. It was so good."

Becca smiled weakly.

"I tried my hand at it, but I could never figure out the egg part." Still moving slowly, I leaned forward and lowered my voice like I was sharing a secret. "They always turned out terrible. I either overboiled them and they became this rubbery, sulfuric disaster, or I undercooked them and the egg whites spilled out over the rice."

The tension broke as Becca and Vicky laughed. The tension in Becca's shoulders released, and she relaxed into her chair.

"So, how long have you two known each other?" I asked.

"Only a few weeks." Becca glanced over at Vicky. "She just moved in. She was the newest resident."

"Wow. Not long, then." I leaned back in my seat and kept my tone even, as if the next question was just as important as their favorite food. "How long did you know Emma?"

Becca lowered her gaze and shifted in her seat. Abby stepped away from the counter and squeezed her shoulder for support. Becca reached up and held Abby's hand while she answered. "I knew Emma for about a year."

"What was she like?" I held still, not wanting to draw attention to myself.

"Nice. Emma was a good person." Becca peered up at me through her hair.

I nodded, encouraging her to continue.

"A few months back, I had gotten into trouble with my mom for missing curfew. It wasn't really my fault. The bus was forty minutes late. I tried to call, but my mom didn't answer. I ran the last two blocks home but didn't make it in time. She said I was a bad example for the other girls. As a punishment, I had to skip dinner and spend time in the detention room." Becca dropped her hands to her lap and fiddled with the edge of the tablecloth. "That's one thing that sucks about being the daughter of Susan and Cyrus Drake. There are a lot of expectations. Emma thought it wasn't fair. It was five minutes, and the bus was late. If it had been on time, I would have been early."

Becca shifted in her seat and was quiet for a while. I let her sit there, not pressing the issue, while she calmed herself.

"That night, Emma snuck into the detention room. She had nicked the keys to the kitchen from my mom and grabbed some of the apple pie I wasn't allowed to eat with the other girls. She sat down on the floor with me, poured way too much caramel sauce over the top, and handed me a spoon." Becca wiped a tear from her cheek. "Emma was sweet. Sometimes a bit too trusting. But she was also mischievous and stood up for what was right."

Vicky squeezed Becca's free hand. "Emma was the first person who welcomed me in," Vicky said. "I always liked her. I felt like we had a connection. My mom raised me, and she was fine. Mostly. But her latest boyfriend, Todd, was a real piece of work. He somehow managed to be worse than my father. Todd only hit her in places where people couldn't see the bruises. When I got the impression he was going to start on me next, I took off. Emma, she understood that pain, and she showed me how it could all be all right in the end."

I fought the urge to ball my hands into fists and grit my teeth. All three of them had had to deal with abusive fathers. I didn't understand the desire to hurt the ones you supposedly loved. The idea of someone doing that to Grace made me furious. And those same abusive men were now in town, acting like they were the victims. "Emma sounds nice. Do you think she was happy?" I asked.

Becca shrugged and wiped at her eyes again. "Sometimes. But she wasn't always."

I needed to understand who Emma was, and starting at the beginning, when she fled from her father, seemed as good a place to start as any. Slowly, I leaned forward and caught Becca's eye. I softened my expression until it was as kind and sympathetic as I could make it. "Like when she ran away?"

Becca clamped her mouth shut and backed away from me. Vicky hugged her arms to herself and looked toward the hallway.

Too soon. Shoot. I've got to regain their trust. I held myself still and filled my voice with sincerity. "It must be hard to trust again. Especially after spending so much time someplace you should have been safe but weren't."

Vicky nodded.

Becca looked from Vicky to Abby to me and sighed. She closed her eyes. "Emma told me that she witnessed something awful, and that's why she ran away."

Something awful? What did David do? I swallowed and kept the same even tone to my voice. "Did she say what she saw?"

Vicky shook her head. "I wish she had."

"She didn't like talking about the bad stuff. I mean, I didn't even know her dad's name until she had been there for six months." Becca said.

"Now no one will ever know what she saw." Vicky sighed.

I fought the urge to slump in my seat. I held myself still, and I contemplated the next question. *How did they end up at Abby's?* I relaxed my jaw, gave them a sad smile, and asked the question.

"Emma wanted to leave." Vicky looked away from me. "After what she saw and then her dad tracking her down...

She wanted to just be on her own. She didn't feel safe anywhere."

"So we snuck off," Becca said. "Emma was my best friend. I wanted to help her. Every year, Abby would send me a letter letting me know I could come to her if I ever needed her. I didn't think he would find her here. And I knew my sister would want to help."

Abby blushed and turned back to the cutting board. "It's what sisters do."

"The ferry was delayed, so we got in after midnight. We walked to the bistro to wait for Abby to come and pick us up. We had been there for about five minutes when we heard it. Something splintering at the front door."

"I'd dozed off in one of the booths. I woke up with Becca's hand covering my mouth." Vicky's voice shook. "It was terrifying. I couldn't see who broke in, it was so dark. We hid behind the counter. That lunatic broke all the lights. He tore the place apart. He spotted us, and... he stabbed Emma."

"That's when my sister arrived. She came in through the back. She grabbed my hand, and we ran. We ran as fast as we could. And I could hear him behind us. When we got to the end of the block, he was less than twenty feet away, I think. It was hard to tell in the dark. But his shape, it was large and barreling toward us. If it wasn't for him tripping over a trash can, he would have caught us."

"If Abby hadn't had her car, he might still have." Vicky shuddered.

"Do you think it was him?" I asked. David didn't live far away. He could have come into town for that and made it home in time for the cops to call.

"I don't know," Vicky said.

Becca nodded. "I can't be sure, but I think so. Emma ran away for a reason."

A silence fell over the table. We all stared blankly forward. The girls were shell-shocked and terrified. Abby continued to cook in the background, her hands moving on autopilot. She glanced back at me. Her eyes had that same haunted look as Becca's.

I'd been chased by killers before. I knew it was terrifying.

"Thank you for telling me," I said finally.

Becca cleared her throat and wiped her eyes. She twisted in her chair and looked at Abby. "So, what's for dinner?"

"Sautéed cabbage and kielbasa over pan-fried potatoes," Abby said.

All our stomachs rumbled. Vicky giggled first, and then the entire table erupted into laughter.

I had asked enough hard questions for the night. I changed the subject to something happier—favorite movies. And we spent the next hour discussing the merits of *Stardust* over a delicious meal. At the end of dinner, they went back downstairs, and I grabbed my purse and headed out the door to meet up with the Retirees for another round of model house building.

In the driveway, the conversation replayed in my head. Becca had sounded so certain that their assailant was hot on their heels. She couldn't be sure of the distance in the dark, but twenty feet wasn't that far. If he was that close, he would have appeared in the footage I got from John.

I pulled out my phone and played the video. Abby ran into view, Becca in front of her and Vicky close behind. They stopped at the end of the block, and Abby stared back the way they had come, and then the group stumbled backward out of view. There was no man. I replayed it again and focused on the trash can that was halfway down the alley.

It shook.

No one was standing next to it, but it shook.

I replayed it a third time. It was about thirty feet from the girls when it shook, but it shook. *Is that David tripping over it? How is he doing that?* I leaned back in my seat. If I couldn't see him with magic, maybe I couldn't see him with technology either. That would explain the lack of prints. He was invisible.

I checked my bag to make sure I had all the notebooks my gran had sent me as well as the one notepad which I had copied the symbol Grace and I found at Abby's diner. I had no idea what it meant, but I was about to go to a witches' school lesson. And if anyone knew, it would be one of the Retirees.

CHAPTER 14

I pulled up outside a massive split-level home and double-checked my GPS. This was the address the Retirees had given me. I had never been to their home before. I stared up at it. The house was both intimidating and adorable at the same time. It was massive, probably at least three thousand square feet. It had a balcony that wrapped most of the way around the building, overlooking their lot. Pansies lined the walkway, and even in winter, the garden beds were full of heather and witch hazel. A trellis covered in the purple flowers of the clematis ran along one length of the balcony, connecting it to the floor. A year ago, I wouldn't have known what any of those flowers were. But over the past few months, Agnes had drilled me on them.

I scanned the street for Grace's car. She wasn't there. I pulled out my phone and texted her quickly.

DANI:
You still on your way?

I sat, waiting for a response for a few minutes. While I waited, I closed my eyes and checked in on Charlie. He was on guard but content. I got the impression he was curled up on someone's lap with his eyes closed to slits so he could still see around him. I checked my phone. Grace hadn't responded, so I grabbed my stuff and marched up their long driveway to the front door. I raised my hand to knock and froze mid motion as the door swung open, and Agnes greeted me. She led me inside to their kitchen. Herbs hung drying over the window, and a butcher block island took up the center of the room. Off to the side was a breakfast nook, where Betty and Sarah were busy unpacking the half-built model from its box.

Sarah glanced over her shoulder at me. "No kiddo today?"

I shrugged and took a seat at the table. "She wasn't home yet when I left. I assumed she would meet me here."

"You look tired," Betty said.

I snorted. "Thanks. It's been a busy day."

"Working or investigating?" Agnes sat down in a chair to my left.

"Both." I pulled out my notepad and phone. "I think there might be a witch involved."

They all turned to me, their jaws dropping in unison.

Betty's eyes widened. "A witch?"

Sarah covered her mouth. "Are you sure?"

Agnes grabbed my arm. "What did you find?"

My gaze bounced from Retiree to Retiree. I loved them, but they were gossipmongers. If I told them Abby was staying with me, everyone in town would know it before noon tomorrow. The only thing I could trust them with was the magic. It was the only secret they viewed as sacred. "Two things, but they're not... conclusive." I showed them the video first and then pulled out the sketch I had drawn of the symbol Grace and I had found at Abby's. I described the feeling of nothing. By the time I was done, they were all squirming in their seats.

Sarah picked up my notepad and squinted at the symbol.

She moved it around and then handed it to Betty. "I've never seen it before."

Betty looked it over next. She held it up to the light and waved the paper to make it move. Sighing, she handed it off to Agnes. "It looks like a combination of symbols to me, but I can't make heads or tails of it."

Agnes set the page down and scurried into the kitchen. She grabbed a pinch of sage and ground it in a mortar and pestle before drenching it in hot water. She strained the mixture through cheesecloth and then pinched her nose and drank the water in one gulp. After that, she returned to the table and picked the notepad back up. The air around her became iridescent as she hummed to herself, staring cross-eyed at the symbol.

I leaned forward, studying the sounds.

After a full minute, she dropped the notepad and sighed. "I don't know what it is. Betty's right. It's a hybrid spell of some sort. The shapes are reminiscent of illusion and protection magic. If I knew what the protection magic did, I could probably piece the illusion part together—but it's connecting oddly. It's definitely magic. An enchantment of some sort. But I'm not sure how it works."

I slumped in my seat.

"We could ask—" Sarah said.

Betty gave her a warning look, and the next words died in her throat.

I straightened in my chair and stared at each one of them in turn. "You could ask?"

Betty grumbled. "We could ask another witch if they know what it is."

"There's another witch?" I inched forward in my seat. My body vibrated with excitement. "Who? When can I meet them?"

"It's not our secret to share." Betty crossed her arms.

I collapsed into my seat again. Of course it wasn't. I

couldn't tell them what color dress I was wearing on a date without it getting out, but another witch. That was sacred. *Maybe they were so bad at keeping secrets because keeping the witch ones took so much work.* I crossed my arms.

Agnes touched me on my shoulder. "But we can see if we can get her permission. She might be willing."

"Okay, ask her," I said.

"Can we show her this?" Agnes picked up my sketch.

I nodded and forced myself to relax. The stress of the investigation was getting to me. I was reacting like a teenager. I straightened, shook out my wrists, and grabbed the model-making tools from the table. "We better get a move on with this if we want to finish it tonight."

The tension at the table eased as we all grabbed our next part of the project. I continued building the framing while Betty added in the popsicle sticks for the walls. Agnes was carefully painting the furniture Sarah had already put together, and Sarah was painstakingly recreating an end table out of matchsticks. We eased back into a rhythm, where we slowly built the model of Meredith's house, one block of wood and tongue depressor at a time. While we worked, Agnes grilled me on the various uses of chamomile. It wasn't only for upset stomachs.

"We still need to collect some dirt from outside the house," Sarah said.

I stared pointedly at my hands as I worked. I didn't want to go back. Meredith's house gave me the creeps. "I don't think I'll have time. The investigation—"

"I couldn't. I'm unlucky. We all know that," Betty cut in.

Agnes snorted. "Why don't we draw straws?"

We all groaned. Agnes was right. It was the only fair way to send someone back to get the dirt.

I grabbed a few toothpicks from the table and broke one in half. I held the bunch out to the group. Sarah pulled first. She got a long one. Agnes reached in second and also got a long one. I held my breath as Betty grabbed one of the last two. It was short.

Betty threw up her hands. "I told you I was unlucky."

"I'll go with you," Agnes offered.

"Well, if you're okay with going—" Betty perked up.

"I said *with* you." Agnes elbowed Betty in the side.

Betty giggled and dropped the broken toothpick on the table. "Fine, we'll go together."

As she said "together," I attached the last piece of the roofing. The last step was a coat of paint. We were almost done.

I glanced at my phone. Grace still hadn't responded, and she was over an hour late. I picked it up and messaged her again.

> **DANI:**
> Are you okay?

GRACE:
Sorry. I forgot it wasn't at our place today.
Go on without me.

> **DANI:**
> We're almost done.
>
> You missed an interesting lecture on the various uses of Chamomile.

GRACE:
I'm sad I missed it. Did you take notes?

> **DANI:**
> Always.

I dropped my phone into my purse and watched as Agnes mixed the paint for the first coat.

"Everything all right?" Betty asked.

"I don't know." I frowned. "The witches' school was her idea. I expected her to be more involved, you know? She's retreating into herself again. And I'm not sure how to coax her back out."

Sarah nodded. "I've been worried too. But I've also been trying to put myself in her shoes. She says she's found peace out in the woods. Can you imagine how hard it is to willingly go to a place that is overstimulating when you've finally found peace?"

"You're probably right," I said.

Agnes finished painting one side and moved on to the next. "Once I'm done with this, all that will be left is the dirt and the spell. On the next full moon, we should have answers about how the curse began."

"And if we have that"—Betty squeezed my arm—"maybe we can reverse it, and you'll have one less thing to worry about with your daughter."

I patted her hand, my eyes welling with gratitude. Getting this curse behind us would be wonderful. If it worked as we hoped, while we would still be witches, the twisting of our powers would be over. Betty could cast spells without something going wrong, Agnes could leave Point Pleasant, Sarah could perform magic any day of the week, and Grace and I could decide when our Sight was active. We wouldn't be in danger of losing our minds to uninvited and unwanted visions. Life would go back to normal. Well, as normal as a life as a witch could be.

CHAPTER 15

Dawn hadn't arrived yet when I pulled up in front of the Bizzy Bean the next morning. Although in mid-March on Whidbey Island, that wasn't surprising. The sun wouldn't be up until after seven, and Heather had sent me an SOS text at five thirty. We had over an hour of darkness left before the town would come to life.

I parked outside the Bizzy Bean. The lights were on in the back. By this time, Heather would have usually been up already for two hours, baking for the morning rush. I let my car idle for a minute while I closed my eyes and sent a querying thought through my connection to my familiar, Charlie. I had left him to watch over the girls in my care. He was half asleep but content. He had begrudgingly gotten up with me this morning and found a comfortable spot to sleep near the girls' bedroom door. If anyone tried to get in there to hurt them, he would hear the intruder. Everything was fine. I released the connection, turned off my engine, and trudged across the sidewalk to the front door of the cafe.

Heather had given me a key, so I let myself in and wandered toward the kitchen. It was quiet. The kittens hadn't been moved downstairs yet.

I found Heather in the kitchen. She was furiously working away at cookie dough, weighing and shaping it into small balls and setting them aside. She worked at a breakneck pace, but she was still only halfway done. I washed my hands in the sink and joined her at the long metal counter that ran down the length of the room.

"Where do you need me, boss?" I asked.

"I overslept. I was supposed to be up at four." Heather grabbed the next piece of dough. "If you could shape the dough into balls, I'll weigh it. I needed to get the cookies into the oven twenty minutes ago."

I grabbed the dough from her hands and started rolling. "Are you okay?"

She both nodded and shook her head as she grabbed another pinch of dough from the bowl and threw it down on the scale. She hadn't had time to brush her hair. Her red locks were balled into a messy, unkempt bun at the back of her neck. Her eyes were bloodshot, and her hands shook as she worked. "Mom couldn't get out of her wheelchair last night to get into bed, so I had to go up and help her."

I winced. Heather was burning her candle at both ends, trying to take care of her mother, run the bed-and-breakfast, and keep the cafe going. "Is she still moving in with your brother, Ash?"

Heather nodded. "Drywall is up. They are painting today and installing grip bars in the bathrooms. He said it should be ready for her in a few more days."

"And then what?" I asked. "Are you still going to be running the B and B and the cafe?"

"I have to." Heather choked out the words as she measured out the next ball of dough.

"No, you don't." I grabbed her hands and forced her to look at me. "Not alone anyway. I'll help where I can, but… promise me, promise me that you are going to hire more help. You can't keep doing this to yourself."

Heather collapsed into my arms and sobbed. "I thought I could do it. I thought, how hard could running a bed-and-breakfast be? My mom's done it for almost half a century. I can't let it fail now."

I rubbed her back and patted her hair. "It's going to be okay."

"How do you know?" She sniffled.

"Call it a witchly intuition," I said.

Heather pulled back and studied my face. She laughed and rubbed at her face, smearing dough across her cheek. "I promise I'll hire more help."

"Good." I bumped her with my hip as we rewashed our hands.

"Thank you for coming. I know you've got a ton on your hands already. How's your investigation going?"

I rolled a ball of dough and grabbed the next one from her. "Not great." I gave her an update, filling her in on my conversation with the girls and my suspicions of another witch being involved.

Heather whistled. "Are you sure it's another witch? Can men be witches?"

"I don't know." I shrugged. "I don't think so. Everyone who's been mentioned so far is a woman. Maybe there are wizards or something? I forgot to ask the Retirees that."

"Did you see David or Cyrus casting any spells?" she asked.

I shook my head.

"Maybe they have a magic item that does it for them. Could a magic item do that?"

I furrowed my brow. I didn't know enough about magical items, but Agnes had called it an enchantment the night before. Enchanted items were part of so many fantasy myths, I had a hard time imaging that they didn't exist. "That could be it. But how would David, Cyrus, or whoever it is, have gotten their hands on something like that?"

"You'll have to ask when you catch them," Heather handed me the next clump of dough. "Let's ignore the magic angle for now and focus on what the next step would usually be. Even with magic, whoever did it would still need an alibi, right?"

I nodded and grabbed the last clump of dough from her. I rolled it into a ball and set it down on the tray. We took turns pushing our thumbs into the centers before shoving the entire tray into the oven to bake.

"What's next?" I asked.

"A ten-minute break to check social media. Let's double-check to see if we can find an alibi for Cyrus or David. And if not… we move on to the next round of cookies."

We rewashed our hands and sat down in a small nook off the main kitchen. Heather poured us both a large mug of her secret brew of coffee, and we settled in to check for alibis.

"Have you thought about having Chris interview Abby? He might know what to ask," Heather suggested.

I shook my head. "He would look at it all wrong. He doesn't know about magic. All he has to go on are her prints being the only ones on the murder weapon."

"The killer could have been wearing gloves, right? Wouldn't that explain it?"

"I don't know."

"You should think about it." Heather squeezed my hand. "I think it's a mistake not to bring Chris in. But I'll support you no matter what you decide."

"Thank you." I squeezed her hand back. "Although I hope that's not just because I'm helping you bake cookies."

She threw her head back and laughed. "It might influence my decision. But no, I trust you. And I think you can trust Chris too. Like you did me."

I closed my eyes and imagined telling Chris everything. I couldn't figure out how he would cope with me taking in

Abby, or me being a witch. *Would he think I'm crazy? Would it scare him?* The bottom of my stomach dropped out when I visualized him rejecting me. I clamped my jaw shut and shook my head. "Not yet. I need more time before I take that leap."

We finished doing our social media sweep. There was nothing there that could be used as an alibi for either Cyrus or David, but that meant nothing. It wasn't unusual to stay off social media after midnight. I would have to figure out another way to verify that information. We put our phones away and got to work on the next batch of cookies while the previous batch cooled on racks.

With only two minutes left to spare, we pulled the last batch of cupcakes out of the oven. I hugged Heather and darted out the door before the opening rush hit. The investigation had eaten up most of my week, and I had a few reports I needed to catch up on at work. I drove a few blocks to my office and got to work.

I had almost fifty unread emails in my inbox when I logged in. I tackled them first, shooting off response after response and updating my schedule for the next week. By midmorning, I had responded to all of them and was busy making phone calls. The front door to the shared lobby opened, followed by the clatter of a dog's toenails against the tile floor. A grin spread across my face. *Did Olivia successfully adopt Bailey?*

I sprang to my feet and scurried to the door. I flung it open as Olivia unlocked hers. Standing primly at her side was Bailey. Her golden fur shone, and she wore a gray-and-red kerchief around her neck that had the logo for both Williams Adjusting and Pleasant View Insurance Agency alternating in the little white squares. Bailey's ears perked up when she saw me, and she wiggled with excitement at the end of her leash.

"I almost forgot how cute she is." I knelt in front of Bailey. She flopped down on her side, presenting her belly for rubs. I happily obliged.

"We thought we weren't going to get her." Olivia pushed open her office door. "Someone else put in an application for her the same day. But luckily, Felicia thought we would be the better fit."

I followed Olivia into her office and took a seat in my gran's old chair. Bailey went to town, sniffing every inch of the office. It was her first time here.

"Charlie will be jealous," I said. "I think he had his heart set on being the only office mascot. But I'm sure I can convince him to share his duties."

"I'll still need Charlie! I'll have to shower him with more toys so he knows he's still got a place here. I only have Bailey in the office on alternating days. That's when Zac works, and Xander will be in daycare. Is Charlie in with you today?"

I shook my head. "Too early of a start to my day. He likes to sleep in."

"You look a little tired." She scratched Bailey between her shoulders as she came over for more love. "You doing okay?"

"Yeah." I stretched and slumped into my chair. "Heather needed a hand this morning. Honestly, I'm glad she called. I need something to keep me busy. Whenever I stop, I can't stop worrying about Abby."

Olivia gave me a sympathetic look and stood. She grabbed a metal bowl and mat from her bag. She filled the bowl with water as she spoke. "You are a good friend. If you need to keep your mind off it, maybe you could help me out with something."

"Anything," I said. "Well, almost anything. I have a few more reports to write, so I can probably only help through lunch."

"It shouldn't take too long." She put the bowl of water down for Bailey. The dog scampered over and inhaled it. "Note to self—walk the dog in twenty minutes. She'll probably need to go."

"Puppy bladders are notoriously tiny. So, what do you need?"

Olivia perched on the edge of her seat, revealing purple argyle socks under the tan pantsuit. "My dad is starting to plan his next phase of his downtown revitalization project. He was thinking about putting in a request for funds to spruce up some of the older buildings but didn't know where to start. Got any ideas?"

Her father, Steven Bishop, was the newly elected mayor. He ran on a platform promising to build back our downtown, and he was taking that pledge seriously. "What about the old sheriff's department? They've been in those doublewides for years. It's about time they got back into their original building."

"I don't know if anyone has looked inside since they evacuated after that water leak." Olivia scrunched up her nose. "How bad do you think the mold is?"

I grimaced. "Growing mold children for its little mold family?"

Olivia barked out a laugh. Bailey pranced around, yipping, her tail going a mile a minute. "Shhhh." Olivia raised her finger to her mouth. Bailey settled back on her haunches. Her tail was still whacking the floor with her excitement. "That's a great idea, though. The department doesn't feel like it's part of the community anymore. Bringing it back into town might help that."

"Exactly." I patted Bailey on her head. She quickly flopped back down onto her side. "And Bob could use all the help he can get on that front. I sometimes think he's forgotten he's part of the community."

Her eyebrow rose, and she gave me a skeptical look. "I

think our sheriff might have forgotten you're part of the community, but... fences can still be mended."

I shrugged. "I'm willing if he's willing." Bob wasn't a bad person, just a vindictive one. He still blamed me for taking away his late wife's hope when I figured out what had happened to their son, who had gone missing over a decade before. Cancer was awful, and her hope might have been the only thing keeping her going.

"It would probably go a long way toward mending that fence if I could mention it was your idea to restore the building," Olivia said.

"Does that mean I'll have to be involved in its restoration?"

"Who better to be involved than a claims adjuster?" she teased.

It was my turn to laugh. Olivia knew me too well. She had known I would suggest the sheriff's office and that she could convince me to volunteer if I did. I held my hands up in surrender. "I'll do it. If your dad can get the funds."

"It's up for a vote in a few weeks." Olivia grinned and swiveled her chair around as she did a happy dance in it. She held up her hand, with three fingers pointing straight up. "And he's already got three city councilmen pledging their support."

"Does this volunteer gig come with any benefits?"

Olivia batted her eyelashes. "My undying gratitude isn't enough?"

"It doesn't pay the bills, but I could make it work."

She swatted playfully at my arm. "Don't worry. It's a government gig. They always pay their bills. Well, almost always."

"I'm on board and happy to help." I gave Bailey one last stomach scratch. "But I've got to get back to work."

"Thank you, Dani." Olivia gave me a quick hug. Her excitement was infectious.

I left her office with a grin plastered across my face as I crossed the lobby. I froze in the doorway of my office. Sitting on my desk was a notebook. And not just any notebook—one of the notebooks from my grandmother. It hadn't been there when I left.

My mysterious benefactor had delivered another one while I was gone.

CHAPTER 16

I dashed out of the lobby and looked up and down the street. I had only been in Olivia's office for a few minutes. There were at least twenty people within a block of the building walking around downtown. None of them stood out to me. I groaned and stomped back inside.

I closed my office door behind me and stalked to the desk. My hand hovered over the book for a few seconds before I had the nerve to touch it. I knew before my fingers landed what I would feel. My heart swelled, and my head felt light. Pride. And something else. *Amusement?* I lifted the book off the table and flipped it open to the last page. In my grandmother's small script it said *5 of 7* in the corner. I dropped it onto the table and spun in place.

Since the last book had been delivered, I had filled the walls with portraits and group shots. There were easily thirty sets of eyes in the room. I walked to the photo with the clearest view of the doorway and touched it. The last emotion was mine. It hadn't been tampered with. I closed my eyes and murmured the words to the spell that would let me relive the object's memory. To work effectively, to truly see the past, the object itself had to be able to metaphorically see as well, either through a camera lens or the image of an eye. Warmth flooded through me as the glow of the spell settled into my skin.

It was odd watching myself leave a room. I smiled softly at the sight. I had a bounce in my step because I was so excited to see Bailey. Less than a minute later, the door opened again. I would have just sat down in Olivia's office. Whoever opened the door didn't step in. Instead, lavender motes of light swirled into the room from the doorway. Half a second later, the room plunged into darkness, almost like it was midnight and the moon was covered. I could make out the outlines of the furniture and the vague shape of someone stepping into the room. Thirty seconds was all it took. The darkness lifted. The person was gone. And the notebook patiently waited for me on the table.

I sighed and released the spell. My plan hadn't worked. *How did they know I would do that?* I ground my teeth and stomped back to the notebook. I flopped into my chair and pulled out my phone to text Grace.

> **DANI:**
> We got another surprise delivered to my office.
>
> Book 5 of 7.

My eyes flicked back and forth impatiently from my phone to the notebook. After ten minutes, Grace still hadn't read the message. I rolled my shoulders and forced myself to relax, one body part at a time, until I was approaching calm. A new notebook meant new spells. And if my prior murder investigations had taught me anything, a new tool for my toolbox. This investigation was proving difficult. *What if there's information on the mark in there?*

I shook my head and checked my phone again. Fifteen minutes and no word from Grace. I turned away from the book and closed my eyes. *We've opened the last few together. I should wait.* I tried to distract myself by sending a querying signal through my connection to Charlie. He was awake and energetic. His joy and exuberance flowed through the connection into me.

I sat bolt upright in my chair. He had the zoomies. Euphoria was not the best emotion for me to tap into at a time like this. It put my impatience into overdrive. I checked my phone one last time. Twenty minutes and no response. *Grace will understand,* I lied to myself as I grabbed the notebook and flipped it open.

I pored through the pages one after the other. This book was intense. There wasn't a single entry that would be helpful in investigating. It was a book on evocation. There were entire passages about lighting things on fire, the dangers involved in trying to change the weather, and how to cool a drink. Halfway through, there was a sticky note covering a spell.

Clever, but not today. You should use this.

I peeked under the sticky note. It was the darkness spell that my mysterious benefactor used to sneak into my office. I chewed on my lip. *Every book had been useful for the case I'd been working on. Every single one. It was like the person knew what to send me.* I stood and paced the room, too afraid to continue with that line of thought. I couldn't cut it off before the question popped into my head. *What if it's my mom?*

Exhaling, I shook my arms out. I jumped in place and fought the urge to continue that train of thought. My mother, Lori, had taken off a long time ago. She wouldn't have cared enough to bring me the books in person. It had to be someone else.

I picked the book back up and tore off the sticky note. I balled the note up and tossed it into the garbage and then fished it out again and carefully smoothed out its edges before tucking it into an inside pocket of my purse. There could be clues on it.

I steadied my breathing and marched into the bathroom. The witch who had dropped the book off had been lucky no one was directly outside when they cast the darkness spell. I couldn't risk any onlookers seeing and freaking out. I closed the door behind me and held the notebook open to the right page. *Okay, I'm going to need this spell for something.*

White motes of light fluttered out of my mouth as I spoke the words. It always amazed me how different magic looked depending on who was casting the spell. Mine were always white, while Betty's looked like floating misshapen pearls. On the second try, the room went dark. To maintain the darkness, I had to continue chanting. I faltered after another six words, and the spell dropped. The brightness pierced at my eyes. I practiced eight more times until I could get the darkness to linger after I said the last words of the spell.

My whole body shook with exhaustion as I shuffled out of the bathroom. I collapsed into my chair and pulled out another protein bar. It had been too long since breakfast, and with all the casting I had done, I was close to depleted. With a snack in my stomach, I grabbed my purse and staggered over to the Slice of Life diner for a proper meal.

Luckily for me, it was just after the lunch rush. I didn't have to wait too long in line for my turn. I put in my order and sank onto a stool at the counter to wait. Willow put a rush on my order and had it out to me within ten minutes. Greedily, I chowed down on my plate piled high with french fries, chicken strips, and fried cheese curds.

The bell of the door tinkled. I glance over between mouthfuls of food. David and Sophia stood at the door, their eyes scanning the crowd. They stopped when they saw me and strode in my direction. I ducked my head and continued to wolf down my food before they got to me. I still had a mouthful of chicken when they arrived.

David stood, staring at the side of my head. Sophia nudged his side, and he glowered. "We wanted to apologize for calling you morbid the other day."

Sophia cleared her throat and nudged him again.

He sighed. "Ever since our daughter was murdered, our old *friends* have been coming out of the woodwork to gawk. I thought... I thought you were another gawker. But after asking around town about you, we found out you aren't. Like you said, you're a friend of Abby's." His jaw clenched at the word Abby.

He didn't continue when Sophia cleared her throat a second time. He closed his eyes instead and breathed in deeply through his nose. Sophia looked nervously between David and me and stepped forward between us. My stomach was still growling, but I fought the urge to shove another french fry into my mouth and held Sophia's gaze instead.

"Do you know where Abby is?" Sophia's voice broke, and she had to wet her lips before she could continue. "All we want is to ask her some questions."

Looking at her broke my heart. Abby was trusting me to keep her, her sister, and Vicky safe. As much as I wanted to say something, I couldn't. I shook my head and tapped the counter for a to-go box.

Willow swooped in quickly and packaged my food while Sophia continued to speak. "Just for a few minutes. Maybe even one. One minute would be enough. We just need to ask her a question."

"I can't help you." I grabbed my to-go box and stood.

Sophia stepped in front of me, blocking my path. She shoved a photo in my hands. My vision swam, and my mouth became too dry to speak. My heart ached. The despair was overpowering. "Please, all we want to know is why Emma was there that night. They didn't know each other. Why was Emma at the bistro? Why did she go to Abby's? What was she doing there?"

"Abby's a good person." I faltered, my hands clenching around the photo. "She would never have hurt Emma."

"Please," Sophia grabbed my hands and stared me straight in the eye. "You don't understand. I haven't slept. Hardly ever since Emma ran away a year ago. And not at all since we got the news. Can you imagine, lying in bed, staring up at the ceiling, wondering when your daughter is coming home, and getting a call like that? I had to hear the words and then repeat them to David when I rolled over to wake him up."

"You were awake?" I whispered. If she was awake, she would have seen David leave the house. I could feel her sincerity through the photo. She wasn't lying. She hadn't killed her daughter. And she had just given David an alibi.

I closed my eyes and replayed the conversation I'd had with Becca and Vicky in my head. I had been so sure Becca was talking about David when she said Emma had run away because she'd "witnessed something awful." But Emma ran away twice. She ran away from David. And she ran away from Cyrus. Emma had seen something awful and run away from *Cyrus*.

David was innocent.

A coldness stabbed into my mind and leached into the edges of my vision. I staggered away from Sophia, my breath catching in my throat. *What was that?* There was a void at the edge of my perception. A void where Charlie had been. It was a distinct nothingness. My heart clenched as the realization hit me. Whoever killed Emma was at my house. My eyes flew open, and I scrambled away from the Wilsons.

"Please." Sophia reached for my arm again.

"Emma was running away from Cyrus," I whispered as I shrugged her off and ran.

CHAPTER 17

Panic filled my mind. I couldn't think straight as I jumped into my car and sped through town to get home. The thought that the killer was at my house and had Charlie repeated in my head every time I tried to calm myself. Cyrus had my familiar. *Did he know what Charlie was? Was he going to hurt him?* In a strange way, I could still sense Charlie. Except it was the lack of him. There was a void in my mind that was Charlie shaped. If he had been killed, I imagined it would feel different. I held on to the hope that he was okay as I barreled past my empty driveway and up the steps to my front door.

It was quiet inside.

The ticking of the clock in the kitchen was impossibly loud. Every footfall as I walked through the living room and to the stairs at the back of the house echoed through the rooms. I paused at the top of the stairs and fished out the pepper spray Chris had given me months before. I didn't know what to expect when I went downstairs. The panic hadn't let me think.

I forced myself to stop and center myself as best I could. *Did I eat enough? Could I even cast a defensive spell right now? I'm so stupid. Why did I waste so much energy on practice?* I shook my head again and refocused. *Charlie needs me. Becca needs me. Vicky and Abby both need me. I can't be going in without a plan.*

I regretted leaving my leftovers from the diner in the car. I backtracked to the kitchen and grabbed a Snickers from the fridge. Grace insisted on having them on hand. It was her favorite pick-me-up. I glowered at the stairs as I ate two of them back-to-back. As I swallowed the last of the bar, I wiped my mouth and returned to the spot at the top of the stairs. I wet my lips and descended.

The quietness felt more oppressive in the basement. Down here, the only sound was my footsteps and my breath. I could hear my heartbeat in my ears as I inched my way down the wall to where the girls had been staying. I pushed the door open with my foot and peered inside.

The beds were unmade, and their clothes were piled into the corner. There was an order to the mess. It was what I would expect a room to look like if three girls shared it. Messy but confined. I stepped into the room, my shoulders tense, and waited. Nothing happened. The girls were gone. Charlie was gone. And I was alone.

I fumbled with my phone and dialed Grace. She wasn't home. *Did he take you too? Please pick up.*

"Hi, Mom," Grace said and yawned.

"Where are you?" I gripped the phone.

"Ebey's Overlook. I was about to take the trail down to the beach. Is everything okay?"

I collapsed against the wall as a tension I had been holding in my shoulders lessened. The situation was bad, but at least he didn't have Grace as well. "I'm working on it. Enjoy your hike."

I hung up my phone. This was too dangerous to drag my daughter into. I paced the room, sliding my fingers over the girls' belongings. There were traces of boredom and a consistent low-level anxiety. I chewed on my lip and backed out of the room. They had mentioned watching TV when we last spoke. I marched back up the stairs. I hadn't noticed it when I came in, but the remote was on the floor in the middle of the room.

My jaw clenched, and my heartbeat quickened. I gasped for breath as my body tried to hyperventilate the second I touched the remote. I felt unbridled terror. I dropped the remote and spun around. There were no signs of a struggle. Just an abandoned remote. I quickly checked the other rooms. My fingers flew over every light switch and door handle. I didn't find anything else weird until I got to the sliding glass door in the daylight basement that opened up into the back yard. That feeling of nothing seeped back into me.

I found the entry point. But it didn't help me at all.

I stood frozen, my mind working a mile a minute, going through the possibilities. The girls weren't here. Time was of the essence. Cyrus wouldn't hold them indefinitely. I had to find them. And I had found Cyrus once before.

My feet carried me back out to my car. I threw myself into the driver's seat and grabbed the maps from the glove compartment. Instead of starting with the map of western Washington, I began with the map of Point Pleasant. I held up the photo of Cyrus's necklace and cast the spell. The lights had never moved so quickly. They bounced rapidly between me, the photo, and the docks.

"Gotcha," I whispered. I pecked out a message to Heather, letting her know Charlie had been catnapped, that the girls were missing, and I was going to rescue them. I threw my phone down on my passenger seat and drove.

A block from the docks, I recast the tracking spell. I opted for the alternate version that laid a path out in front of me, and I followed it from the parking lot to the row of vehicles waiting to board the ferry. Cyrus sat behind the wheel of an older-model white Lincoln Town Car. He spotted me and climbed out, a wide smile on his face.

"Miss Williams, imagine seeing you here." Cyrus's smile widened even further. "Are you having a good day?"

I ground my teeth and forced a smile as curious onlookers peeked out their windows at us. "Peachy. I was just looking for my cat. You wouldn't happen to know where he is?"

Cyrus shrugged.

I stepped closer to him and dropped my voice. "Where are they?"

"Where are who?" He raised his eyebrows and pulled out a pack of cigarettes.

"You know who I'm talking about," I hissed.

"I haven't seen Abby." He hit the back of the cigarette pack against the palm of his hand to knock one loose. "But I'm happy to let you check my car if that would make you feel better."

I lunged forward and grabbed his hand. My fingers brushed against the pack of cigarettes. Warmth radiated through my body, and my chest expanded as I inhaled deeply. I had expected to feel nothing. To be vindicated in the void that was his emotions, but instead, I was greeted by his smugness.

Abby's mom climbed out of the car and circled around to stand next to him. The young girl who had the sides of her head shaved popped out next. They stood on either side of Cyrus, concern in their eyes. "Is everything all right, dear?" Abby's mom asked.

"I was just going to show this nice lady the trunk." He sauntered to the rear of the car and popped it open.

It was cavernous, but there wasn't a single item in the entire trunk.

My hand darted out to touch the car. The warmth returned

but stronger. Cyrus was even more smug than he had been before. He was amused and knew exactly why I was there. I worked through the possibilities. *He's working with someone. But who? All the people I've seen him with are here.* "Who has them?"

"If I knew where Rebecca or Victoria were, I would tell you." He closed the trunk and leaned against it.

I forced my hand to linger on the car. Holding it there and feeling his joy at my frustration almost sent me over the edge. "If you hurt them—"

"You have it all wrong." The young girl stepped between us.

"Mackenzie," Cyrus said, a warning note in his voice. The smugness was replaced with annoyance.

"He wouldn't hurt them, and they know it." Mackenzie crossed her arms over her chest.

"If they know it, then why did they run away?" I asked, my eyes locked on her face. I held my hand steady. The annoyance in Cyrus had shifted to anger, and just under it, there was fear.

"That's enough, Mackenzie. We need to board soon. Get back in the car." His words were clipped.

"Why? It would help if she knew. If Vicky was afraid of Cyrus, then why did she tell him they were safe and not to worry about them this morning? I heard him talking to her."

Cyrus's panic spiked. He stepped away from the car, cutting off my connection to his emotions. "In the car, Mackenzie. Now."

Who is he working with? My mind landed on Robert, Vicky's father. Even as I thought his name, I struggled to picture his face. Robert had been at the memorial. He had been in the Wilsons' room before I found the letter. And the fact that I couldn't remember what he looked like cemented my suspicion that Robert was the killer. *But why? Vicky said her dad wasn't a nice man. Maybe this is what she meant. But she couldn't have known Robert and Cyrus would work together. Her fear back at the house was real.*

I gritted my teeth and stepped back as the speakers blared, announcing boarding. There wasn't anything I could do to stop Cyrus from getting on that ferry without causing a scene. And he didn't have the girls—or Charlie. Robert did. And having an altercation with Cyrus would hold him at the docks as much as it would me. I had to let him go. For now. My legs shook as I retreated from the boarding area.

"It was nice talking to you, Miss Williams," Cyrus called out to me. I hunched my shoulders as he laughed.

I focused on my breathing as I walked back to my car and slumped in my seat. A locator spell didn't work on a person. The only way I had found Cyrus was through his necklace. I didn't know what the girls were wearing. I straightened in my seat. But I knew what Charlie was wearing. He always had his orange collar on with the words *indoor cat* stitched into the fabric. I could still feel the void in my mind where Charlie should be. *If I can't find Charlie, maybe I can find his collar.*

I grabbed my phone and quickly found a photo of him. It was easy. I took one every time I saw him doing something cute, which was at least fifteen times a day. Finding a photo with his collar in view was harder. I scrolled through a few shots before I found one that would work. His white face and trusting blue eyes stared out at me from my screen.

"Your mama's coming for you," I whispered. I zoomed in to see the collar and cast like my life depended on it.

CHAPTER 18

Every muscle in my body tensed as I threw all of my will into the spell. The motes of light flew out of me and swirled around the car like a whirlwind. They plunged into the photo of Charlie and winked out one by one. I clenched my fists and tried to force the locator spell to work. The lights streamed out of me, faster and faster, until the inside of the car looked like a tornado. But no matter how much I threw at it, no matter how much I struggled, the lights vanished as they flew into the screen.

My vision swam. I dropped the phone as the muscles in my arms gave out. I collapsed and slid down my seat until my knees were resting against the steering wheel column. My head pounded. I could barely move, my arms were so weak.

I had done it. I had overcast and depleted my reserves. Through pure force of will, I kept my eyes open. I stared forward at the clock. *What is wrong with me? I'm acting like a reckless fool. Think the problem through. I am not a hammer. This problem is not a nail. In one minute, I am going to reach over and grab the leftovers.* I breathed in through my mouth and out through my nose as I counted down the seconds.

I was still weak, but taking a minute to calm myself worked. My hands shook as I reached over and grabbed the leftovers. I still had a mountain of french fries, two pieces of chicken, and a hunk of fried cheese curds that had glommed together into a sticky mass. My stomach rolled. Cold leftovers weren't the most appetizing, but it had to be done. I started with the french fries first. It was an easy carb to refuel.

With food in my system, my thoughts cleared even more. For the past hour, I had been operating on adrenaline and fear. I sighed. It was like all the lessons I had learned over the past six months about dealing with tense situations had flown out the window the second someone took Charlie. Since he had become my familiar, I had come to rely on the warmth of his presence in the back of my mind. But it wasn't just his absence I was responding to. There was a trickle of fear and desperation coming in from somewhere. *Are we still connected?*

I grabbed my purse and flipped through the notebooks. The fear was bubbling under the surface, and I knew I couldn't push it aside for too long. I had to find a way to harness the fear instead. I looked through every spell. The books were no use for that. I shook my head. I was trying to work around the fear like it was a witch problem, but it wasn't a witch problem. It was a human problem. A problem every mother faces when her kids are in danger. Charlie wasn't just a cat. He was my familiar, and I cared about him in a similar way to Grace or my grandmother. He was my family. "And what do I do when I'm scared for a family member? I reframe it."

I closed my eyes and analyzed the frightened thoughts. *Losing him is a real possibility. Acting rashly makes that possibility more likely. So will anger. But determination? That I can do something with. I am determined to get him back—them all back—and I need help to do so.* I moved on to a piece of chicken as I pulled out my phone and dialed Betty.

The phone rang three times before Betty answered. "Dani—"

"Emma's killer has abducted Abby, her sister, Vicky, and Charlie." I barreled through her greeting, not giving her time to speak. "I tried to track them by locating Charlie's collar, but it didn't work. I need your help figuring out a way around whatever spell this guy has protecting him, and I need that help now before any more innocent people die."

"He has Abby?" Betty croaked.

"And her sister, Becca. And Vicky." I pushed the fear down and forced it to reshape itself into determination before I said the next words. "And Charlie."

"Where are you?"

"The docks." My hands shook, so I hung up before my voice betrayed me. I knew Betty would come. She had promised my gran to take care of me, and she never broke a promise if she could help it. It was just a matter of time before she pulled up with the other Retirees in tow.

I stared at my phone. There were a ton of missed text messages from Heather.

> **HEATHER:**
> Catnapped? Where are you? Do you need backup?
>
> Dani? What's going on? Are you okay?
>
> If I don't hear back from you soon, I'm calling Chris.

I suspected whatever help the Retirees had to give would involve a lot of magic, and Chris wouldn't understand that. The last message was sent less than a minute ago.

> **DANI:**
> I'm at the docks. I'm safe. I've called in reinforcements.

My stomach was still growling, so I grabbed the glob of cold cheese curds and munched on that while I waited.

It felt like an eternity before Betty arrived, but in reality, it was less than thirty minutes. I got out and watched as she parked and the Retirees poured out of her truck. As always, they wore matching tracksuits, except today their jackets were mismatched, like they had grabbed the first things they put their hands on in their closets. Agnes hugged an over-sized sweater to herself, while Sarah looked almost comical in her puffy jacket. Betty opened the rear passenger door, while Sarah ran to the trunk and pulled out a plastic step stool. She placed it gently in front of the open door. I stared at Agnes, Betty, and Sarah quizzically as another woman climbed out.

The woman was about my age, maybe a few years older. Her dirty-blond hair was pulled back into a loose ponytail, and she wore loose black slacks and a mauve turtleneck. She leaned out and braced her forearm crutches on the ground before taking a tentative step down. There was something vaguely familiar about her. It took a moment to place her. I hadn't seen her in years. She had been a few grades above me in school, so I used to see her hanging around the boardwalk with her friends when I visited for the summer.

"I'm Dani." I stepped forward and extended my hand.

The woman glanced between me and my hand and read-justed her crutches. She held her hand out. Her grip was light, and she winced at the pressure of my hand. "Kimberly Jones."

Jones? I wracked my brain trying to think of where I had heard that name before. There was the obvious saying—keeping up with the Joneses—but this felt more important. My eyes widened. "Are you a descendent of Lillian Jones?"

137

Lillian had been one of the members of Meredith's coven. If Kimberly was a descendant, it meant she was another one of the cursed witches like me.

"Yes." Kimberly narrowed her eyes. "I have no interest in discussing the curse with you. I only came because my kids love Abby, and I don't think I could look them in the eye if I didn't act and something bad happened to her."

My jaw dropped. *Did I do something?* I clamped my mouth shut and nodded. She was here to help. My questions could wait. "Thank you for coming."

Kimberly nodded and hobbled forward. She pulled out from her pocket the notepad I had left with the Retirees with my drawing of the symbol that Grace and I had found at Abby's diner.

"You were right in your assumption that it wasn't one symbol," Kimberly began.

The Retirees gathered around her as she sketched. I fought the urge to cross my arms over my chest and moved to the other side to watch.

"It's two symbols that have been combined until they have an almost symbiotic relationship. I can tell that the first symbol is a protection sigil. It's fairly standard, although this one has been modified somewhat. I believe the intent is to make the wielder difficult to trace. The second one, I'm not as versed in." She sketched the second symbol and flipped it around so everyone could see.

Agnes nodded. "As I suspected, somebody cast an illusion spell. The symbol is modified too, but not well. The illusion covers what's there, but instead of replacing it with something else, the spell is trying to make it invisible. That's the nothing you've been feeling, Dani. A better invisible spell would blur things with the background instead."

Sarah picked up the papers. "Maybe the illusion portion of the spell had to be simple so the symbols could work in concert. The more complex the spell, the harder it is to keep going. If whoever designed this wanted the spell to have a persistent effect, something would have to give on the complexity side. I can't see how you make the protection side less complicated, but nothing versus a blur? It may have been more desirable for the caster to erase any trace of themselves than to risk looking like a weird blur on camera. That would get noticed."

"How are we supposed to find someone who leaves nothing behind?" I asked.

"Because"—Betty's eyes brightened with hope—"no one is supposed to leave nothing behind."

"That's right." Agnes bounced with excitement. "The lack of a trail is a trail in and of itself."

"What?" I furrowed my brow.

"Every living thing leaves something behind. You should know that better than anyone." Sarah grabbed the notepad and ripped out a blank piece of paper. She tore it up into tiny pieces and scattered them in a cluster on the hood of my car. "But when someone doesn't"—Sarah slid her finger through the pieces of paper, leaving a trail behind—"there is a trail of nothingness. Outside of outer space, there shouldn't be a spot where nothing exists around here. There are too many people. Too many living things. Too much emotional residue scattered everywhere you look."

My heart skipped a beat as hope surged through me. They were right. I had figured out where the killer had been based on the absence of emotion. If we could somehow track that, we could find him.

"What type of tracking spell do you use?" Kimberly asked.

"I have two." I grabbed the second notebook that my gran had left me out of the car and flipped to the pertinent page.

"I think we can work with this. We need to invert the intention, so instead of looking for something, we are excluding things." Kimberly tapped the page.

Invert? Turn the intention upside down? The possibilities

boggled my mind. That was next-level, highly advanced witchcraft she was throwing around. *I'll have to add that to my questions for a future witches' school lesson.*

"We would want to add in a range limiter as well," Sarah mused.

Kimberly glanced at the spell in my notebook as she scribbled something down on the notepad. "Like that?" she asked.

The Retirees clustered and crossed things out and re-scribbled. The notepad went back and forth between them until it came to a sudden stop in Kimberly's hands.

"This should work." Kimberly smiled and then hunched over the trunk to transcribe the scribbled mess into something more coherent. She handed it to me.

There were similarities between the tracking spell I had used before that laid a trail out in front of me. But there were so many differences between my old spells and the new one. At first, it was hard to see how they were related. The longer I stared at the new spell, the more sense it made. It was elegant and had a style different from everything my gran had written down. This spell had the flavor of five different witches working together, and it was glorious.

"Okay." I shook out my arms and raised the notepad in front of me.

Agnes grabbed my arm. "You look tired."

"The spell has to get done." I straightened and tried to look strong. The trembling in my fingers gave me away.

Betty gave Kimberly a pointed look.

Kimberly sighed and grabbed the notepad from me.

"What are you doing?" I asked.

Kimberly pointed at me and then at each of the Retirees in turn, jabbing her finger forward with each word. "Don't get any ideas about forming a coven with me. I'm not interested."

Agnes held up her hands.

"This is for Abby. It's a one-time thing. That's all. Are we clear?" Kimberly's eyes narrowed as she glared at us.

"We're clear," the Retirees said in unison.

"Does this mean you're going to help me cast the spell?" I choked out.

Kimberly glowered. "I am helping Abby." She dropped the notepad onto the hood of the car and angled it so we could all see. She leaned forward on her forearm crutches and held out her hands.

"Thank you." I gently took her left hand.

Agnes took her right hand, and Betty slipped in between Agnes and my car. Betty leaned against the hood and reached out for my hand. I stretched to grab hers as well. Sarah gripped my shoulder in solidarity. The moon wasn't full, so she was powerless to assist, but it felt like she wanted me to know she still cared. Once all our hands were linked, we chanted.

Kimberly led the chant as Betty, Agnes, and I funneled our magic into her. It was beautiful. Betty's oddly shaped pearls danced through the air that had taken on an iridescent quality from Agnes. My motes of light chased the pearls around. Kimberly's magic looked like red-tinged globes of metal that had a slight coppery scent. I glanced at her. Her face was paler by the second. *Is that blood?* The thought startled me, and I almost missed a beat. Betty squeezed my hand, and I refocused.

The magical energies swirled together, creating a mini vortex in front of us. Kimberly released my hand and reached forward to grab on to the light.

My mouth fell open as I stared.

"Don't stop," Sarah whispered into my ear.

I swallowed and continued chanting as Kimberly physically held the lights in her hand. She clenched her fingers around them, forcing the lights to become condensed and thinner, until it was almost like a strand of pure energy flowing between her fingers. *What is she doing? How is she...?* I didn't know where to start with my questions. I had never seen anything like it.

With the strand of energy between her fingers, she pulled a small rock from her pocket and tied the thread of energy around it. The rock glowed and pulsed under her fingers. As she tied the last strand of magic, the Retirees stopped chanting. I faltered to a stop after them, staring slack-jawed at the glowing rock in Kimberly's palm.

"What..." I stammered.

"It's the easiest way to get a spell to stick around so you don't have to continue chanting forever." Kimberly shrugged and handed it to me. "It'll only last until nightfall, though, so you better get a move on."

I had learned more in the last twenty minutes than I had in two months at witches' school. It pained me knowing that I wouldn't be able to ask follow-up questions or have another lesson with Kimberly. At least not until I figured out why she didn't like me. I didn't remember ever having done something to her.

I closed my fist around the stone. There wasn't a path set out in front of me. But farther down the docks, there was a pillar of light streaming over a sailboat. That must be where Robert was keeping the captives. I grabbed my last protein bar. I inhaled it as I rummaged around in my purse for the pepper spray and a handful of zip ties. I used two to attach the stone to my belt loop, and I shoved the others into a pocket, just in case.

Kimberly was a powerful witch, but by the way she had winced when we shook hands, it was clear she was no fighter. The Retirees' curses made it so they couldn't help either. Not with this next stage. Sarah couldn't cast magic until the moon was full, and any spell Betty cast on her own went horribly wrong. By the way Agnes blanched when she saw the boat, I was pretty sure her restriction on leaving Point Pleasant extended to the water. This, I would have to do alone.

"Wish me luck." I strode toward the docks.

CHAPTER 19

I followed the pillar of light out into the marina. There were rows of docks that stuck out into the water. The light came down on a sailboat at the end of the very last row. I held the pepper spray in one hand and padded toward the boat, my eyes scanning the surroundings. Almost half the boats were missing for the day. The next ferry wasn't due to arrive for another hour. Only a handful of cars had arrived to wait. There wouldn't be a crowd there for at least another thirty minutes.

The light on the security camera in the last row was off. I glanced between the cameras above the other rows. The camera hanging over the last row was the only one that was out. I peeked around the corner of the boat shed at the end of the dock to a trail that led straight to this section from the woods. Robert had thought ahead. He would have been able to get the girls onto the boat without a single camera showing them.

I swallowed and inched down the dock. The wood creaked under my feet. The scent of sea salt and fish filled my nose and mouth. While I had ridden on the ferry over a hundred times, I had never been on a sailboat before. The thought of being out at sea, the water roiling beneath me, turned my stomach.

I exhaled shakily through my mouth and then inhaled slowly through my nose. Until my heartbeat slowed, I repeated the pattern. *I can do this. The Retirees know where I am. Worst-case scenario, they can send in reinforcements, right?* I gripped the pepper spray as I took the last few steps to the edge of the sailboat.

It looked to be at least thirty feet long. The lights in the cabin were off, but the pillar of light was landing straight on it. The light flowed into the cabin doors and disappeared inside. I tensed and then jumped toward the boat, grabbing on to the railing.

My time at the gym had paid off. After my encounter with Jessica's killer, I had taken up jogging, and after my encounter with Jim's killer, I had taken up weightlifting. I wanted to be able to lift myself if I ever had to. It had taken a few months of consistent work, but I had managed my first pull-up the week before. My fingers ached as I dug them into the wooden beam. I grunted as I hoisted myself onto the ship. I rolled to the cabin wall and crouched near the doorway, straining my ears to listen. In the distance, seagulls cawed. Tiny waves hit the side of the boat and broke. Other than that, it was silent.

I steadied my breathing again, and then crab walked through the door. There was a short flight of steps down. I took them slowly, carefully transferring my weight from foot to foot to avoid making any noise. Once inside, the tracking light became diffuse. Robert had been to so many places inside the boat that the light had a hard time settling over any one location. The entire space radiated nothingness.

Keeping low, I padded down the hallway, checking each door as I went. The first door led to a bathroom. It was clean and tidy. Everything had its place. I closed the door and moved on to the next. It was a storage closet, filled with bedding, dry goods, and rows of cleaning supplies, duct tape, and heavy-duty trash bags. I swallowed. *That's not creepy.* I slid the door closed and moved on to the next area.

The hallway led into an open space that was a kitchen, living room, and dining room in one. It was sparsely decorated, with an almost-cheery naval theme. An oar with cute fish hung on the far wall. The table was bolted to the floor, with a white crocheted lace tablecloth draped over it. Everything was tidy and clean. There was a faint scent of bleach. My breath shook, and I pushed the fear down again as I inched across the room to a set of doors on the far wall.

I twisted the doorknob. It turned and then stopped sharply. The door was locked. *Shoot.* I took a step back and stared at it. I hadn't successfully performed the spell to unlock a door yet. Manipulating forces was not my strong suit. I could force the door open, but it wouldn't be delicate. I didn't have any fancy words or a spell to draw on. Just my intent. Wetting my lips, I held my hand in front of the doorknob and blew out motes of light. I slammed my will into the lock, and the door cracked.

Something creaked behind me. I gasped and rolled to the side, already murmuring the words to the darkness spell. The wood splintered as a bullet struck where my head had just been. A second later, the room plunged into darkness.

I froze where I landed and blinked until my eyes adjusted.

The room wasn't as dark as I expected. But that was because the light from the tracking spell still glowed on every surface, with the exception of the few places I had touched. A path of my emotional residue cut through the room, keeping those areas dark.

Robert stood in the middle of the room, holding a gun in front of him with both hands. He glowed brighter than the rest of the room, and brighter still was a cord around his neck. Seeing him now was odd. For the first time, I could really focus on his features. He had light-blond hair, with a trimmed goatee and piercing blue eyes. His features were sharp. Without the effects of the spell to protect him, he was a striking individual. And he didn't look anything like Vicky.

He inched forward through the room, feeling ahead of him with his foot. I fought back against the fear that had left me plastered against the floor and forced myself to sit up. Shaking, I rose to my feet but kept my head low. I widened my stance and padded around him. Before I could rescue the girls, I needed to get that gun away from him. His eyes were wide, and he cocked his head to one side, listening. I froze. He turned in a slow circle, searching with his ears, trying to find me.

Both of his hands were on the gun, and I needed him to let go with one of them. I breathed shallowly to minimize the sound of my breath and slowly moved myself into position. I lowered myself even further, until I was about mid waist, and raised the pepper spray to my left and above my head.

Robert screamed as the pepper spray got into his eyes. He fired again on instinct and then removed one of his hands from the gun to wipe at his eyes. I dropped the pepper spray and lunged. With one hand, I grabbed the gun, and with the other, I gripped on to the ring around his neck. I threw myself backward with all my weight, pulling the gun and the ring with me. As my back hit the floor, I immediately rolled to the side. The gun slipped out of my grasp and skidded across the floor.

Robert immediately went dark. I couldn't see him anymore. The talisman still glowed in my hand, but the room was also dark. The only thing that glowed now were the spaces where I had been since I had taken the ring from him.

He stomped around the room. "Do you have any idea what you've just done?"

The sense of Charlie returned. And with it, access to my familiar's senses. The glint of Charlie's eyes caught my attention. He was standing where the locked door had been. Charlie stared up at Robert, and through his eyes, I could see.

Robert was kneeling and grabbing something attached to his ankle. My heart skipped a beat. *He has another gun.* I surged to my feet and grabbed the oar from the wall. Robert raised his pistol as I hit him hard on the side of the head.

He fell backward.

I stood over him, my breath coming in ragged gasps. Robert wasn't moving. He still breathed slow, steady breaths. And blood oozed from a wound in his head. The door behind Charlie creaked. My head snapped up.

"Who's there?" Abby stood in the doorway, staring wide-eyed into the room, her hands still bound in front of her.

"It's me." I crossed the room to the light switch. I put my hand on it and dropped the darkness spell.

"Dani?" she croaked. She stared between me and the unconscious man at her feet. She let out a shuddering breath and covered her mouth.

"Where are Becca and Vicky?" I asked.

Abby snapped to attention and looked behind her. "In here. Could you help untie us?"

I undid her bonds first, and then helped her loosen the ropes around Becca and Vicky's wrists. They flung their arms around my neck and wept with gratitude. I collapsed to the ground and held them as best I could. My arms and legs were like jelly. Charlie rubbed his head against my arm. I dropped my hand, trying to pet his head, but I didn't have the energy. Charlie shoved his way under my arm and pushed his way into the middle of the group. He pressed his head against my neck, under my ear. My chest vibrated with the power of his purrs. The surge of adrenaline was fading as relief flooded through me. I had found the girls in time. They were safe. Charlie was safe. I buried my head in his fur and cried along with the girls.

"I was so scared," Becca whimpered.

"You're safe now," I murmured between sobs as the girls continued to grip my arms.

"Who was he?" Vicky sobbed.

"You don't know him?" I asked.

Vicky shook her head.

"He's not your dad?"

"My dad's dead," Vicky said. "He was killed in a boating accident off the coast of Alaska years ago."

Another lie Robert, or whatever his name was, had told. *Was anything about him real? How did he know to masquerade as Vicky's dad? Cyrus must have told him to.*

Abby looked over at the unconscious man. "How long do you think it'll be before he wakes up?"

I didn't know. This was the first time I had knocked someone out. "I have zip ties in my pocket."

Abby fished the zip ties out of my pocket and tied Robert up while I continued to hold the girls. She called 911 and then we sat together, only half hysterical from the ordeal, until Harrison from the sheriff's department arrived.

CHAPTER 20

The door to the Slice of Life diner closed behind me. It was still unusually busy, but Heather and Abby had managed to snag a table in the back. I made my way through the crowd, gave them both a quick hug, and sagged into the booth across from Abby.

"I'm glad to see Bob released you," I said. The sheriff had taken her into custody when he arrived at Robert's sailboat two days ago.

Abby shrugged. "For now. I think he's still planning on filing charges against me for hitting my abductor with the oar. He's claiming assault and battery is still assault and battery, even if it is in self-defense."

"You didn't have to confess to that." I squeezed Abby's hand. "I'm the one who did it."

"I know that." Abby squeezed my hand back. "But you were only there because I was stupid enough not to go to the cops to begin with. I figured the sheriff was going to hold me for questioning anyway, so… why make things bad for my rescuer?"

"Did they figure out why Robert killed Emma?" Heather asked.

Willow stopped by the table to take my order. I'd had a late lunch, so I wasn't particularly hungry. I ordered a peanut butter and banana milkshake. She then stepped to the side to tidy up the condiments station.

"He was an assassin," Abby said.

I gaped at her. *A hired gun? In Point Pleasant? That's hard to believe.*

Abby nodded. "From what I heard through the walls while I was being held at the sheriff's station, Cyrus had too many kids in his care. He was shoving in ten kids per room and claiming to social services that each one had their own space. When one of the kids threatened to turn him in, he killed them. Emma witnessed it. She stole a bunch of incriminating documents and ran off. When Cyrus realized what she had done, he panicked. He reached out to a buddy of his, who knows a guy who knows a guy, and they hooked him up with a hitman."

"Wow." Heather slumped against the bench, her eyes wide. "How did the cops find out?"

"Emma mailed the proof to her social worker, Nora. It just arrived yesterday. That, and the hitman is rolling over on Cyrus. I didn't think hitmen did that. But after his arrest, extradition orders started pouring in. His real name is Vincent, or something like that. The guy's wanted in eighteen different states, so he's willing to testify if it means they don't ship him off to Texas."

"I didn't think they had any evidence on this guy," Heather said.

I coughed. "Someone must have fixed the technological glitch that was messing up the reading of his prints. It's the weirdest thing."

"I'm glad the glitch was fixed." Heather eyed me.

I furrowed my brow and leaned forward. "If she witnessed the murder, why did Emma write a letter to her parents claiming she was happy?"

"Becca said Cyrus has all his new residents write that letter before they get moved into the shared rooms. He keeps the letters in case their families come sniffing around," Abby said.

"That's sick." Heather shook her head and picked up her glass of lemonade. "To two evil men going to jail."

"Two bad guys and one wicked woman." Abby lifted her glass.

"Woman?" I asked.

"My mom," Abby said.

"Oh, Abby." Heather grabbed Abby's hand and squeezed.

"Don't feel sorry for me. Not for that." Abby squeezed her hand back. "My mom got what she deserved. She helped Cyrus despite knowing what he was like. She knew what he had done. And she helped him. Like she had since the day we arrived at his home when I was a kid after my parents divorced. She chose him over me, over Becca when she was born. Over kindness. She chose him over being a decent human being. I'm glad she's finally facing the music."

"To facing the music." I picked up my water, and we all clinked cups over the middle of the table. "How are Becca and Vicky doing?"

"Okay, I think." Abby lowered her gaze. "Vicky's going home to her mom. Apparently, her mother broke up with her boyfriend, so it's safe there now. It's going to be a rough transition for her. She still blames herself for keeping in contact with Cyrus after they ran away. But she didn't know what Emma saw and… fell for his charm. It's a mess. Becca is mad at her, and I can't blame Becca for that, either. She's been betrayed by almost everyone in her life. I've convinced Becca to stay with me for now. I'm in talks with her social worker about becoming her guardian. If she's going to learn how to trust people again, she'll need to be with someone who cares. It scares me a little, but I still feel guilty that I left her behind all those years ago when I ran away. I was only seventeen, but she was a little kid. I should have done more."

"You did what you had to." I patted her hand. "You had your father to go to. She didn't. It wasn't the same situation. And now that she is old enough to decide on her own, you're here for her. And that's what matters."

"I am just hoping I can find something to keep her busy." Abby sagged onto the bench. "If she's anything like me, she'll want to keep busy. Stopping to think is stressful."

"Becca doesn't happen to have experience working at a cafe, does she?" Heather asked.

Abby perked up. "Actually, she does."

Heather sipped her lemonade. "Well, I'm hiring. If she wants the job, it's hers. And if it helps get things back to normal quicker for everyone, then it's a win-win all around."

"I don't think things are going to get back to normal anytime soon." Abby sighed.

"Why's that?" I asked.

"I'm losing my lease." Abby scrunched up her face as tears formed at the corners of her eyes. "They say I'm a bad risk now. I mean, I still have my food truck in storage. So it's not all gone. So long as I can find a place to cook."

"You can cook in my kitchen," Willow said.

I jumped. I had forgotten Willow was standing at the condiment stand. She hadn't moved to turn in my order and instead had been standing there listening. I could understand her hesitance to move away. A post-investigation wrap-up conversation was the most interesting thing she would hear all day.

Abby's face broke into a smile. She wiped at her eyes and beamed. "Really?"

"Really." Willow nodded. "You're my biggest rival at all the food competitions this town has. It wouldn't be much fun if I won all of them."

"You really are a good friend." Abby stood and pulled

Willow into a hug. "I will happily be your rival at the next bake off."

The door to the diner opened, and Willow glanced at the door. "I should probably stop snooping and get back to work. Come by at six a.m. sharp, and I'll get you set up."

Abby nodded and stepped back. We watched Willow as she glided across the room. It was people like Willow who made me love living in Point Pleasant.

My eyes slid past Willow to the person who had opened the door. It was Chris. I hadn't seen him in a few days. He hadn't been at the station when Harrison brought us in for questioning. I slid out of the booth. "I should probably go say hi to Chris."

Abby and Heather nodded and returned to their conversation about Becca working at the cafe. Iris, Heather's mom, was leaving for Ash's place in two days, and Heather could really use the help at the cafe. Abby was calling Becca on her cell phone as I left the table.

I sidled up next to Chris as he waited by the counter for his food. "Hey, you." I slid my hands around his arm. "My schedule has opened up if you are ready to schedule that rain check."

Chris looked down at me and then glanced at the table I had come from, his expression pained. "Why didn't you tell me about Abby? She was at your house, and you never told me."

"I promised her I wouldn't," I said.

Standing that close, I could see the hurt in his eyes. "You promised to keep me in the loop on your investigations. You know I've always supported them."

"I—"

"Maybe I was just hoping a promise to me would mean more." He slipped out of my grasp.

"I'm sorry." I tried to catch his gaze, but he wouldn't look at me. "What can I do to make this up to you?"

"I don't know." He shrugged. "For the past week, all you've wanted from me is information. I'm going to need time to think about it."

My eyes watered. "Chris, you know how I feel about you."

"Do I?" He stepped away from me and collected his order from the counter. Without another word, he turned and trudged out of the building, his shoulders hunched and his eyes averted.

Did he just break up with me? My legs wobbled, and I followed him out. I didn't have the strength to go back to the table. Everything had been going so well, and... I messed it up. *There was magic involved. I couldn't have told him anything. He wouldn't understand. He would have gotten into trouble with Bob. I did the right thing, didn't I? There was magic involved. Magic.* I fled to my car and threw myself into the front seat before the tears started. *I'm a witch. There's always going to be magic involved. I can't expect a relationship with him to work if he doesn't really know who I am. But I want it to.*

CHAPTER 21

Tears streamed down my face as I drove home. *What am I supposed to do now? I don't want to lose him. Chris is the best thing that's happened to me since the divorce.* When I pulled up to my house, Betty's truck was parked in the driveway. I sat in my car, sobbing as I tried to get control of myself before walking inside. It was a full moon tonight, so Sarah could access her magic. We had been planning all week to cast a spell on our model of Meredith's house. It couldn't be rescheduled, even if I had a broken heart. I got out of the car and climbed the steps to my front door, my arms wrapped around me.

Betty, Sarah, and Agnes were waiting for me, with the box of the model at their feet next to the door.

"I lost track of time," I murmured as I pushed the front door open. I shuffled to the kitchen and collapsed onto a chair. My mind was still on Chris. *How do I get him back?*

Agnes studied my face. "Are you okay?"

I shook my head. "How do witches stay in relationships?"

They exchanged a look and took seats around the table.

Sarah sighed. "They don't."

Agnes put her hand over mine. "Or they learn to live with the lies."

Betty scoffed and pushed Agnes's hand away. She picked my hand up and stared at me until I met her gaze. "Or they are lucky enough to find someone they can be themselves with. Not everyone runs."

"How do you know if you're lucky?" My voice cracked.

"You just know." Betty squeezed my hand. "And I know Chris loves you. So why not take the chance?"

"I don't know if he even wants to talk to me again," I cried. "I think he just dumped me."

"Trust me, sweet pea." Betty stood and pulled me into a hug. "He wants to talk to you. I promise."

I clutched on to her as the sobbing overtook my body. "How can you know that?"

"I've seen the way he looks at you." Betty stroked my back as I gripped her. "This is just a blip in the road. Everything is going to be okay."

The Retirees sat in silence as I cried. After a few minutes, the surge of emotion faded. Despair could only hold my thoughts for so long before I became numb to it out of self-defense. At least for now. I was sure I would cry again in another hour. I had a lot to think about, but now was not the time. We were on a time crunch. Deciding what to do about Chris could wait until the morning when I had time to sleep on it.

I pulled back and wiped my eyes. "We should probably get started. I wouldn't want to waste the full moon on me moping."

They chattered together as they unpacked the model of Meredith Walker's house. Betty fished a bottle of dirt from her bag and sprinkled it in a circle around the base of the house. While they worked, I checked the time. Grace should have been home by now. It was well past dinnertime. She knew this was happening tonight. I texted her and waited.

My mind kept returning to Chris. I closed my eyes. I had to find something else to think about while I waited. *Robert's ring.* I stood and retrieved it from my bag. "Have you ever seen something like this before?"

I handed the ring to Agnes, and she turned it over in her hands. She passed it to Sarah next, and then it went to Betty. They talked over each other as they inspected the ring. It was hard to follow. I let them talk, my eyes tracking the ring as it went from woman to woman.

"It's an enchanted ring," Agnes said at last.

"I got that," I said. "Did the killer make it himself?"

"I doubt it." Betty handed the ring back to me. "There are some wizards out there, but the magic on this thing is old. Older than me old. He either inherited it, or he bought it off the black market. My money's on the black market."

"There's a black market for magic items?" My jaw dropped. It made sense. Some of the stolen items I had come across over the years while handling claims were odd. There was a market for almost anything. *But magic items?* "Wouldn't the Counsel be upset about that?"

"Oh, they are." Sarah crossed her arms.

"Rogue magic items are like half of what they deal with, from what I've heard," Betty said.

I stood and put on the kettle for tea. My mind was going a mile a minute. *Was the Counsel going to be coming for the ring? How did they track the items down? Was I going to be in trouble for having it? How did non-magical individuals even use the items?* My hands shook as I put the kettle down on the stovetop. "How have I not heard about any of this before? Wouldn't people notice magic items floating around?"

"Magic never makes the news as magic. It's always... gas leaks or something like that." Sarah stood to help me with the tea. "Plus, who would expect to have a magic item like that here? All the sightings I hear about in the US are in New Orleans, the Great Lakes, or someplace in Georgia where the magical communities are a lot more active."

I handed out mugs, and we sat and drank the tea in

silence. I didn't know what to ask next, so I filed my thoughts away. The day had been too long and too weird to continue with that line of questioning today. Just like my decision on what to do about Chris, that would have to wait for another time. We had a spell to cast.

I checked my phone. It had been half an hour since my last message, and Grace still hadn't responded.

"Do you think we need Grace?" Agnes asked.

"She's better at looking into the past than me," I said.

"We can wait a little longer." Betty stared at the door.

I glanced between the three women seated at the table. We had all waited long enough. And if the spell didn't work, I didn't want to get Grace's hopes up for nothing. The four of us might be strong enough to do it.

"No," I said. "Let's do it now."

We moved the model to the center of the table and joined hands around it.

"You have the power of divination, Dani, so we are all going to hand our power to you," Sarah said. "Are you ready for it?"

I swallowed and nodded.

I started the chant. Sarah picked it up, and then Betty and, lastly, Agnes. With each new chanter, the energy thrumming through my hands increased. My body vibrated with energy. It was unlike anything I had ever felt before. I held my eyes open and continued chanting, fighting past the overwhelming flow. With my mind, I willed the spell to behave. *Let me see. Let me see how this curse began.*

I felt as if I was falling. My vision swam, and suddenly I was standing in Meredith's living room. The colors were muted, and things shifted oddly as I moved my head. Meredith entered the room. Her honey-blond hair, with a single silver streak at her left temple, hung in stylish waves. She wore a red pencil skirt with a matching jacket. I backed myself into a corner and held still as she opened her front door.

Six women pushed past her into her house and shut the door behind them.

"What are you doing here?" Meredith asked the women. Her voice echoed strangely. The image shifted and rolled, like a pebble had been dropped in a pool of water.

I couldn't tell which of the six women spoke. It was as if they all spoke at once. "We are here because of you. We know about your deal. It needs to stop."

"I can't stop." Meredith's mouth didn't move, but I knew it was her speaking. "If I back out now, I'll lose everything."

The vision kept rolling and shifting, like something was trying to buck me off. I gritted my teeth and pushed forward with my mind. *Show me what I came for.*

"If you don't back out, the Wardens will come, and all of us will be blamed. We can't let that happen. Do it, or we'll strip you of your powers." Again, the voices of the women came as one.

"Break the law to hide my indiscretion?" Meredith laughed. "You would do that to me? One of your sisters?"

"It's for the greater good." One of the women stepped forward. She looked vaguely familiar. The Retirees had called her Ruby.

"Selfish! You're all selfish!" Meredith wailed. She threw up her hands, and green sparkles flew from her fingertips.

Another woman slammed her foot into the ground, and the sparkles bounced off an invisible force field. *Was that Lillian Jones?*

Meredith continued to scream. The green sparkles flew faster and harder against the barrier. Lillian slid a foot backward. She leaned into it, the muscles in her neck bulging. Wind picked up in the room, lashing at everyone.

"She's too far gone," Ruby yelled over the howling wind. "We have to do it now."

They ducked their heads against the wind and shuffled toward each other. The women encircled Meredith and grabbed on to each other's hands.

"Traitors!" Meredith screamed. "Selfish traitors! You've let them take everything from me."

Who? What did they take? What deal? I gritted my teeth and focused my will again as the room convulsed around me.

The green sparkles flew faster and faster until I could barely see Meredith standing in the middle. The women gripped on to each other and bent their knees so the wind wouldn't blow them over. They started chanting. Blue lights came out of the mouth of Edie Williams, my ancestor. Those lights were joined by dancing flames, beautiful shape-changing globes of energy, floating metal stars, flower petals, and an iridescent fog that flowed between it all.

The walls of the house spasmed, and my vision swam again. *Not yet. I will see it. I will see what happened. Show me!*

The green sparkles erupted and slammed into each of the women. Their grasp on each other broke, and Edie went flying back into the wall.

Lillian stomped her foot again, and the force field went back up. The women threw themselves back into a circle and continued to chant.

"You can't do this to me." Meredith slumped to the ground. "Traitors... Traitors..."

The green lights winked out all at once, and Meredith crouched on the ground, shaking.

"I don't think the containment is going to hold for long," Ruby said.

"We should contact a Warden," Edie suggested. "We confined her. Wouldn't they take that into account?"

"Traitors... Traitors..." Meredith whimpered.

"Can we risk it?" Another woman asked. I tried to focus on her face, but it was hard as the vision convulsed again. *Is that Clara? Agnes's mother.*

"May all your dreams turn to ash." The white streak in Meredith's hair spread, and her eyes took on a green glow. She climbed shakily to her feet and raised her hands again. A single green mote of light formed on her fingertip.

"Watch out!" Ruby screamed.

Meredith flung the green mote from her finger. The light divided into six and hurled straight at each of the women gathered. In a split second before the mote struck, Beatrice Taylor, Betty's grandmother, screamed and hurled her shape-changing orbs into the center of the room. As the orbs struck Meredith, they sank into her skin and pulled her down to the ground. Her skin became woody. As she melded with the floor, the purple lights exploded. The lights hit every woman in the room, including Meredith. She wailed as she became part of the house.

"May all your dreams turn to ash." Meredith's voice echoed as she disappeared.

I opened my eyes. At some point during the vision, I had fallen from my seat, and I was lying on the kitchen floor. *What did I just see?* I sat up and crawled to my seat.

"Did it work?" Betty whispered.

I nodded.

I replayed the vision.

Meredith had green sparkles like Grace. *Weren't Grace's sparkles purple once? When did they change color?* My eyes flew open wide. The color of the sparkles changed after Grace got that splinter during our first foray into Meredith's house. They had been becoming more purple, week by week. I scrambled to my feet, ran into the living room, and grabbed the second notebook I had gotten from my gran. On instinct, I flipped it open to the page with the tracking spell. I had used it so many times by now, I knew where to find it in an instant.

"What's wrong?" Betty scampered after me as I bolted out the front door.

Without a word, I grabbed the maps from my glove compartment and walked back into the house. I threw the atlas down on the couch and flipped to the page with the map of Point Pleasant.

"What happened?" Agnes stood on the other side of me.

I couldn't stop now. I had to know where my daughter was. She wouldn't have missed this. I knew what my daughter's car looked like. It was emblazoned in my memory. I didn't need a photo for reference. I stared straight at the map as I spoke the words to the locator spell. The motes of light flew out of my mouth and quickly landed on the page.

My heart sank.

Grace wouldn't have missed this, but Meredith would. Grace's car was outside Meredith's house. I didn't know how. I didn't know why. But somehow, Meredith had her.

"Isn't that Meredith's house?" Sarah stared at the map.

I nodded.

"Who's there?" Betty whispered.

We all knew. It was obvious by who was missing.

"My daughter," I said.

Can't wait for the next book? Book 6, 'Grimoires and the Ghostly Guest,' will be coming out January, 2025. Be the first to uncover the next magical mystery in the 'A Williams Witch Mystery' series. You can find my other books by scanning the QR code below:

In Book 6, Dani Williams is no stranger to mysteries, but when a maid at Bee's Bed and Breakfast is found dead, her divination powers spiral out of control. Piercing headaches and relentless visions haunt her, demanding she uncover the truth.

She quickly realizes there's more to the guests at the B&B than meets the eye. Hidden agendas, suspicious behavior, and elusive clues make every suspect look guilty. With the pressure mounting, she must work quickly to uncover the truth. But as she digs deeper, her personal life is also unraveling—Grace's strange behavior grows more concerning by the day, and her relationship with Chris hanging by a thread —Dani is forced to juggle far more than just

Secrets, supernatural encounters, and buried truths await in this captivating paranormal cozy mystery. Can Dani solve the case before her Sight—and her life—falls apart completely?

JOIN MY NEWSLETTER

Interested in receiving bonus content like inspiration character art or a free short story? If so, scan the QR code below to become a member of my mailing list and receive access to fun things like 'Foresight and the Fateful Ferry,' a free short story. Go on an adventure with Dani and Chris as they journey to Seattle for a fun day out, and things take a dramatic turn when they stumble upon a dead body on the ferry.

ABOUT THE AUTHOR

Eloise Everhart lives in the Pacific Northwest. Her childhood was marked by voracious reading and tabletop roleplaying games, fueling her lifelong passion for storytelling.

By day, she's a dedicated insurance adjuster. It's a career that has honed her sharp eye for detail and developed her inquisitive mind—a skillset she now seamlessly integrates into her cozy mystery writing.

Beyond her storytelling ardor, Eloise is a devoted wife, sharing her home with a menagerie of rescued cats and dogs who have found their furever home in the Everhart household.

ACKNOWLEDGMENTS

I am thankful to my editors, Rashida Breen and Darlene Gardner, for working with me to piece this tale together. Their thoughtful comments helped forge a messy first draft into its final form.

To my husband, Nate, you make me feel like the luckiest woman in the world. You support me in my dreams. You encourage me on the days I feel down. And you help me get back up every time I stumble. There are no words to describe how thankful I am to have you standing by my side.

To my sister, Andrea, and my parents, Chas and Tammy. Your love and encouragement in my formative years inspired me to embrace my creativity, and I am forever thankful for that foundation.

My deepest gratitude goes to my readers who have joined me on this journey. Your enthusiasm inspires me to continue the tale.

And as always, in memoriam of my best friend, Andrew. If it was not for you, I would not have rediscovered my joy in writing after college. You relit the fire inside of me, and your memory continues to drive me forward.

"Come on a journey with me."